Praise for
A Babysitter's Guide to Monster Hunting #1

"This shining gem in the campy-monster-drama genre
is a step up from R.L. Stine's Goosebumps."

—*School Library Journal*

"A series opener that melds Goosebumps and the
Baby-Sitters Club with ironic glue."

—*Kirkus Reviews*

"This new series gives babysitting a daring edge and
sets up girls outside of the popular crowd as heroines.
An entertaining debut."

—ALA *Booklist*

ALSO BY JOE BALLARINI

A Babysitter's Guide to Monster Hunting

A Babysitter's Guide to Monster Hunting #2:
Beasts & Geeks

...ide to

MONSTER HUNTING

3

MISSION TO MONSTER ISLAND

Joe Ballarini

Illustrated by Vivienne To

KATHERINE TEGEN BOOKS
An Imprint of HarperCollins Publishers

Katherine Tegen Books is an imprint of HarperCollins Publishers.

A Babysitter's Guide to Monster Hunting #3: Mission to Monster Island
Text copyright © 2019 by Joe Ballarini
Illustrations copyright © 2019 by Vivienne To

Library of Congress Control Number: 2019934618
ISBN 978-0-06-243791-4 (pbk.)

Typography by Joel Tippie
21 22 23 24 25   PC/BRR   10 9 8 7 6 5 4 3 2 1
❖
First paperback edition, 2021

For the bad kids with good hearts—
I'll see you in detention.

1

U R so ugly.

#MISTAKEFACE.

Do the world a favor and disappear 4 EVER.

Standing at my locker, I stared at my phone in shock. The comments were everywhere: my 'Gram, 'Book, Snapchat, the Twits. Even the three YouTube videos I made two years ago had gotten flamed.

I didn't recognize any of the screen names on the comments, and I didn't want to look them up. I was afraid I might see someone I knew.

I glanced at the kids rushing to class. Anyone could have written this awful stuff.

What did I ever do to them? I couldn't help it if I was born with uncontrollably awesome frizzy red hair and a geeky smile.

My phone buzzed again. New comments shredded the selfie I took of Berna Vincent and me in Mathletes.

> Die, Carrot Top, die.
>
> This girl is such a nothing.
> A big fat ZERO.

I jabbed my thumb into the power button and shut my locker, wondering if I should just delete all my social media.

"Girl, someone is trolling you. Hard," Berna said, walking up to me.

I cringed. "You saw?"

"If I don't have your back, who's going to have mine? I looked up the accounts. They all seem to be finstas. And for the record, I *like* your freckles. You have a galaxy of them."

I smiled. Berna was the best. I linked my arm with hers, and we set off for class.

Red hearts were scattered all along the hallway. On the walls. On the windows. A banner decorated with glittering hearts and fat cupids hung over our heads like a looming spirit.

"If these hearts weren't made of paper, we'd be walking through a total massacre," I said. "Eeesh. I meant that as a joke, but it came out superdark."

"That's what Valentine's Day feels like," Berna sighed. "Some baby in a diaper with a bow and arrow shoots you in the back and leaves you for dead."

"I'll be your valentine, Bern." I put my arm around her. "I'll even go to the dance with you."

"Puh-lease," Berna said. "You're going with Victor."

Victor Ramon and I were sort of a thing. I guess. I mean, we kissed once. But that was a couple of weeks ago after I almost died fighting Serena the Spider Queen over Christmas break. Serena was upset that I had vanquished her brother, the Grand Guignol, just a few months before on Halloween. All totaled, I had nixed two of the seven deadly Boogeypeople with Victor's and the babysitters' help. I could have taken down the third, Professor Gonzalo, but that mad Boogey-scientist got away after I was bitten by the Spider Queen.

Victor and I had spoken a lot about that night's crazy events and how much he wants to join the Order of the Babysitters, but there had been no mention of the Kiss. Either he was too nervous to mention it or it didn't mean that much to him.

Or he thinks of me like a friend.

"He should have asked me by now," I said.

Berna plucked a cardboard heart from a wall of hearts and looked down at it like it was a rose on *The Bachelor*. The Valentine's Dance was a legendary event at Willow Brook Middle School. It's not exactly prom, when the guy asks a girl in a supercreative way and then picks her up in a limo and it's this huge deal, but somehow it still felt epic.

"When I was in the fifth grade," Berna said, "I heard an older girl whispering to her friends how her life changed forever after her first real slow dance."

I nodded. "I want butterflies to lift me off the ground like in musicals and take Victor and me to our own private kingdom in the clouds."

"I don't know about all that," Berna said. "I'm just saying it'd be fun to go. I'm not trying to sound snobby, but the boys at this school are one step away from raccoons in a dumpster. We're on a different level. And that's cool, but that means I've got no one to dance with. And I don't want to turn out like my mom. All work, no play. That woman's crazy."

Berna's mother, Flo, was proud to be an ex-babysitter who had chased a few monsters in her day. Flo actually wanted Berna to become a babysitter warrior, and she was like an overbearing Dance Mom but with monster hunting. Flo had Berna studying monster medicine since the age of eight. And she made her run an obstacle course full of rope swings, climbing walls, and a kiddie pool full of leeches in their backyard every morning before school.

Flo was letting us use her house as our temporary babysitter HQ since our old HQ was burned to the ground by Professor Gonzalo and the Spider Queen. Flo insisted we use her house rather than the Boston HQ because it was less of a commute. We dearly missed our old wondrous babysitters' paradise. It was three hundred years old and held a ton of history, and one of the Boogeys' monsters just torched it. On the bright side, Berna's mom was really happy to have her own house full of babysitters and monsters.

The banner for the Valentine's Day dance swayed gently under the wind rushing from the students heading to class.

"It would be fun to go," Berna said. "I got this dress my mom won't let me wear to church. It's all purple and cute."

"Done. You and me. We are going to this dance. Together. I mean it, Bern. Sisters before misters. Ponies before bronies. Girls before squirrels."

Berna giggled and leaned her head on my shoulder.

"Okay," she said. "But I want a ton of chocolate and candy."

"So do I," I said.

"And flowers. And a giant stuffed teddy bear, holding a little heart, that says 'I wuv you' when you squeeze it."

"Don't push it, sister," I said.

Berna winked. "Don't trip on that stuff online. Those are just dumb comments written by haters."

"I know," I sighed. "Sticks and stones. But it still hurts."

Deanna and the Princess Pack floated past. They were giggling at something on Deanna's rhinestone-bedazzled phone. I glared.

"You think it was your frenemy?" Berna whispered.

"I don't know. Deanna's online shade skills are limited to single words like 'sad' or really dumb phrases like 'boo-hoo 4 yoo hoo.' Or emojis she manages to make insulting."

The princesses whisper-giggled in my general direction.

"What's so funny?" Berna said, crossing her arms.

"Call a fireman, Kelly. 'Cause someone is burning you," said Deanna.

"Did you write that stuff?" I asked. "If you did, can you delete them? Like, now."

Deanna gasped, hand to her heart. The princesses stepped back, suddenly offended.

"Why would I make up like a dozen fake screen names just to waste them on your social?" Deanna stepped closer. "Kelly, if I ever bother to burn you, you will know it was me. But c'mon"—her smile was as venomous as a pit of snakes—"you have to admit. They are kind of funny."

I bared my teeth.

"Don't be such a snowman in the sun. These trolls are stupid losers with nothing better to do. You should be grateful for the attention. It's driving your page views up. Not that I'm jealous. I'm not. I am a good person, and I do consider you a friend. Even though you're, like, still mad at me for Tammy or whatever."

Tammy had been my best friend since forever—until a few months ago when forever came to an end. We didn't have a huge fight or breakup. I started hanging with the babysitters and Tammy started wearing makeup and hanging around Deanna and the Princess Pack. We drifted.

But Tammy hadn't hung out with Deanna since

Christmas. Lately, I saw Tammy hanging out with the art kids in Mrs. Danube's art room. She'd traded in her princess pinks for dark and brooding blacks. Now she takes superserious photographs of, like, dead birds. My mom says Tammy's still trying to find herself.

"Tammy is such a spazz-o," Deanna said. "She thinks her posts are all deep and moody, but they're just disturbed and weird. She's turned into a total creeper."

"Stuff a sock in it, Deanna. Tammy's awesome," I snapped.

Even if Tammy was my ex-best friend, I wouldn't have anyone bad-mouthing her.

"We're going to say good-bye before I bop this girl in the nose," Berna said, pulling me away.

SKREET! SKREET! SKREET!

Earsplitting alarm bells shrieked. The rush of kids jolted. Emergency lights flashed. A stampede of teachers with bad ties, comfortable sneakers, and itchy wool skirts rounded the corner.

I stiffened. The back of my skull tingled.

Berna narrowed her eyes. "Lockdown," she said.

P rincipal Wing's tense voice came over the PA system: *"Attention, students and faculty. Calmly
and quietly, proceed to your nearest assigned safety
zone."*

A sea of sixth, seventh, and eighth graders broke
into giddy chaos.

I nervously unzipped my backpack and removed a
can of Pringles, which hid my collapsible babysitter
bo-staff. Our sitter senses were on high alert.

A squealing sixth-grade squirt elbowed past me.

"Watch, it!" I yelled. "And get to your zone, little
man!"

Berna and I escorted a few lost sheep into their
classrooms.

"Miss Vincent and Miss Ferguson!" yelled Mr. Brown. "Stop dawdling."

Berna waved her walkie-talkie. We always kept them handy in case we didn't have a cell phone signal.

"My safety zone's in room 301," she said before darting off. "Call me!"

My safety zone was room 610. Way at the butt of Hall C on the other end of school.

As I passed the boiler room on the way to Hall C, the shrill alarm stopped. The air was empty and oddly quiet. A few stray kids ran behind me, and soon the echo of closing doors and hurried sneaker squeaks stopped, and I was alone in the halls. The flashing emergency lights kept blinking.

My footsteps echoed. Something felt off to me. I slowed down, listening to the silence.

An urgent voice came from around the corner, along with the shoe squeaks of authority.

"I don't know what it was, but I know I saw something." Our lunch lady, Mrs. Francini, was waving a spatula and a rolling pin. She walked briskly alongside the school security guard, Mr. Milo.

"I was in the kitchen, elbow-deep, mixing a bucket of meatloaf. There was a clang. Can you slow down, please? My sciatica."

I curled myself into a Hide-and-Seek–bouncy-ball

position as they breezed past me.

"This—this—thing was there. It wasn't no schoolkid neither. It was a bear, I guess. Scared the boogers out of me. Must have been eight feet tall."

"This is the third time this month," Mr. Milo sneered.

"You're telling me," said Mrs. Francini. "Darn thing ate all my nuggets!"

Mr. Milo and Mrs. Mystery Meat sped down the hall.

I knew it! *This isn't a normal lockdown situation. This is a monster situation.*

I glanced in the window of the door to room 610. Kids were huddled against the walls on the floor, sitting still. Mr. Gibbs had begun the check-off list. Soon, he'd be calling for Ferguson, K.

I clicked on my walkie-talkie to channel three.

"Team. This is Firebird. Repeat, this is Firebird. Do you copy? Over."

A pop of static. "Go for Queen B. Over," whispered Berna.

"Casshie ish go," said Cassie McCoy in a hushed tone.

"Critter on the line" came Curtis Critter's eager voice.

"You've got to shay 'over,' Curtish. Over," scolded Cassie.

"Cassie, don't be–"

"Shee? Over! That way we know when you're done talking. Over."

"You're messing it up–"

"Like that. Over."

"Cut it out!"

"Fine. Over for real!"

"Over infinity!"

"This is ridiculous–"

I was about to fill them in when I saw the lock on the boiler room door. Someone–*something*–had slashed it. Inch-deep claw marks raked across the open door.

"We've got a situation," I whispered into the walkie. "Over." At this point normal, regular, *smart* people would run and scream for the security guard.

But not me. Not Babysitter Kelly Ferguson. I gave up on normal a while ago.

The sound of the hinges on the boiler room door scraped like nails down a chalkboard as I pushed it open. An old metal staircase led down into the guts of the school. Among hissing pipes and machinery, a single light bulb glowed in the dark, dungeony basement.

"Firebird, you there? Over," Berna said. "Wait for backup! Over."

"One sec," I said. "Over."

It's tough to see in the dark. But not for me. The best way I can describe it is like squinting until a muscle in the back of your eye pulls into your skull, and suddenly, you can see in the dark. (It helps to have extrasensory babysitting powers.)

13

I spotted small brown pellets on the bottom steps. I crouched down.

Please, don't be monster poop. I don't have any Baggies on me.

Chicken nuggets with huge bites taken out of them.

The lunch lady's fried delights were splattered with ketchup and puddles of saliva. A small trail wound down the steps and across the concrete floor, vanishing into our school's rusted underbelly.

Water gurgled in the pipes like the school itself had indigestion.

"We've got a Class Four, possibly Class Three, in the boiler room," I whispered into the walkie. "Over."

I popped the lid off the Pringles can and slid out my babysitter bo-staff. As I panther-stepped toward the mass of pipes, I snapped the staff to its full length. The whoosh it sang while I spun it was music to my ears. I had been training with it for a month now.

A sound of a gruff swallow followed by lips smacking came from behind the boiler.

My muscles coiled. I pointed the staff.

"By the order of the Rhode Island chapter of Babysitters, I hereby order you to leave the premises," I said.

The boiler chugged. Pipes rattled.

"You are surrounded by babysitters. We know you're down here."

I held my breath and raised my weapon, accidentally

14

knocking it into the light overhead. The light bulb bounced on its chain. Shadows swung around me.

Through the noise of hissing pipes, I heard deep, throaty breathing.

I thrust up my staff. Steam exploded from a broken pipe. A cloud of mist blinded me. Black claws shot from the fog and grabbed at me. I cracked my staff across huge, gnarly knuckles.

The giant paw pulled away. I could hear pathetic whimpering through the smoke. I squinted through the haze.

"Ooooaaaaww" came a bellowing cry.

I know that whimpering.

"Kevin? Is that you?"

An eight-foot-tall, furry Sasquatch with twisted horns emerged from the mist.

FRom A Babysitter's Guide to
Monster Hunting

NAME: Kevin LeRue

TYPE: Human mutated into monster

AGE: 14

ORIGIN: Mutated on Monster Island

STRENGTHS: Keen sense of smell, superstrength, running, leaping, sign language

WEAKNESSES: Limited vocabulary, gets HANGRY, sometimes forgets he's no longer human

The cord from the headphones plugged into his long, droopy ears ran down his chest and into a blue and gray fanny pack strapped to his waist. He was holding his paw, mumbling to himself. I let out a sigh and retracted my snake staff.

"Sorry, dude. Didn't know that was you," I said.

"Meee murrr?" Kevin said.

"Well, I can't think of any other monster it would be, either, but you can't sneak up on me like that."

He nodded and looked genuinely sorry for scaring me. "Awree."

"Your paw okay?" I asked.

Beast-Boy waved me away like "it's cool" even though I could tell I had really hurt him.

"What are you doing here?" I asked.

He held up a science textbook.

"You want to go to class?"

He smiled a mouthful of shiny tusks.

"Kev . . . ," I said gently. "You know you can't be out in public like this."

He nodded and stared at his big feet.

A long time ago Kevin was a human kid and brother to my friend Liz, the most kick-butt babysitter in Paw-tucket, but he was changed into a monster by Professor Gonzalo and used as a servant by Serena the Spider Queen. We freed Kevin from the Boogerpeople's—I'm sorry, *Boogey*people's—clutches, and ever since,

Monster Kev's been hanging out with us at babysitter HQ in Flo's house.

We had been getting Kev used to being back in the human world. Playing football with him even though it takes five people to tackle him. We've been learning sign language to understand him better, and we even got him to agree to a shower once a week. The way he smelled, he needed a shower twice a day, but once a week was a start.

The more we hang out, the more I can see underneath his layers of fur and snarl to a sweet, fourteen-year-old guy who loves animals, his sister, and all kinds of music. We've caught him sneaking out to 7-Eleven in the middle of the night. Two weeks ago he snuck into a night club just to rock out. Ever since he showed up, there have been a lot more bigfoot sightings.

But he's still really clumsy and has terrible anger issues and poor personal hygiene. Basically, a teenage boy.

"School's on lockdown because of you," I said.

Kevin kicked the ground. He offered me a chicken nugget.

"No thanks," I said. He tucked it into my pocket. "Quit messing around."

In his other paw, the beast held up a red cut-out heart.

"What's this?" I asked.

17

His hairy eyebrows raised. *Will you be my Valentine?* he signed.

I smiled.

"That's very sweet, but we need to get you out of here," I said.

His hairy arms whirled around, and he pointed a claw to his forehead.

"What? Kevin, we have to go. What are you saying? You remembered something?"

"Oot, oot," Kevin said, circling his paw.

"Something about the mixing bowl? The swirl in the sea. The island? Something about Monster Island!"

Kevin pointed at me and then to his snout.

We had been gathering intel ever since we found out there were still missing kids trapped on the island where Kevin was turned into a hairy mutant beastie. These were kids who had been stolen away from their parents by real monsters. Some kids were waiting to be turned into creatures like Kevin; others had already been transformed. I'd promised myself, Kevin, and those kids that as soon as we located the island, the babysitters would bring them home.

I had no idea how I was going to do any of this. I just knew in my gut I had to do it.

Kevin unzipped his fanny pack and rummaged through pens, leaves, and a dead mouse until he found a folded paper. Over the past few months, Kevin had been drawing every little detail he could remember about Monster Island. His drawings were crude fragments, small clues we hoped would help us with our rescue mission. However, we still had not been able to locate it. One of the biggest clues he gave us was that the island was run by the deadliest of the seven Boogeypeople, Baron von Eisenvult.

FROM A Babysitter's Guide to Monster Hunting

NAME: Baron von Eisenvult, aka the Wolf, aka the Baron, aka the Big Bad Wolf
TYPE: Humanoid wolf; Class 1; leader of the seven Boogeys
STATUS: Living in exile
LIKES: Sheep and human hamburgers
STRENGTHS: Power and ruthlessness; great sense of smell; a keen eye for accounting and business; razor-sharp claws that can slice a babysitter in half with the flick of a wrist; jumping, fencing, basketball (Is there anything

this monster can't do?); incredible hearing; excellent nautical skills; impeccable taste in art and fine wines

WEAKNESSES: Narcissistic and sociopathic behavior. Isolated. His own selfish greed? His endless hunger for vengeance?

WEAPONS: Claws, swords, blades, knives. HIS BITE.

HISTORY: This ruthless leader has no problem tearing children from their families for his own gain. He sees humans as if they were lesser animals and he is the top dog. The Wolf has led many attacks on humanity (see the War of the Five Tentacles, and the Eldritch Battle, on page 64) but has since gone unseen for a few years.

WARNING: Do not pull his tail. He hates that.

Kevin gave me a drawing of what looked like a building with a circle around it. "ELL" was written on the side of the building.

"Ell? What's 'ELL'?" I asked.

Kevin grunted and gestured, like he was looking out of a window.

"You saw this. Out of the window? On your way to the island?"

Kevin threw back his head and howled.

Ugh. Monsters. Once they start howling it's hard to

get them to stop. I clamped my hand over his mouth.

"I'm glad you remembered something important, but the Willow Brook Middle Search Party's gonna hear us."

Shadows appeared under the door to the hallway. Slowly, it creaked open.

"Hide!" I said.

I shoved him behind the boiler. His horns clanged on the metal pipes. Kevin's breath huffed onto the back of my head. I shivered and elbowed him to back off.

"Awbarree?" he grunted, pointing to my hair.

"Yeah. My shampoo's Strawberry Zest. Now be quiet."

Footsteps clanked down the metal stairs. I held my breath. Mr. Gibbs had for sure realized I was not in attendance and had sent teachers with torches and pitchforks to come and get me.

Please, please, please don't be the principal or the security guard.

If an adult found us, they would flip out. They'd call animal control, and animal control would lock Kevin up and experiment on him. Or they'd claim to have found bigfoot in our school basement, and every nut-job in the world would want to throw him behind bars so they could gawk at him.

Of course, I would never let that happen. Which means I would have to cause a major scene so Kevin could escape—which would probably land me in detention. And I, Kelly Ferguson—flawless, gold-star student—do not get detention. Especially since I'd made a deal with my parents: I could be a monster-hunting babysitter as long as my grades were good and I stayed out of trouble.

"Kelly? You in here?" Berna whispered.

I jumped out from my hiding place. Kevin followed my lead and leaped out with a happy roar. Berna squealed and threw her flashlight at me.

"That is not funny!" she scolded. "I could've killed you."

"Sorry, Bern. I didn't think you'd come looking for us," I said, hugging her.

"What are babysitters for?" she said. "And you, big guy. You know you're not supposed to be out right now. Wugnot's going to have a cow so hard he's going to start mooing." Wugnot was our hobgoblin babysitting buddy. Since he was trying not to eat humans, he was pretty strict about following the rules.

Kevin nodded, swung his hairy arms around the two of us, and squeezed until the air whooshed out of my lungs. He nuzzled our faces with a long purr.

"Yeah, yeah. I'm happy to see you, too, but that's enough," Berna wheezed. "The whole faculty is headed this way."

"We're being hunted!" I said. "Kev, we have to get you out of here."

We scrambled up the stairs. Eyes wide on the empty hallway.

"Nearest exit's the end of Hall C," I whispered. "Quietly. I'm talking to you, Kev. You need a bath, by the way."

Kevin sniffed his overgrown armpit and snorted.

We hustled down the corridor, crouched below the windows in classroom doors.

Curtis turned the corner. "Wait! Don't go this way!" Curtis shriek-whispered. "I had to create a diversion for the teachers. This way!"

Elbows and knees in rigid military formation, Curtis bolted, like he was running a race for the Dorksville Champion Cup.

"What about the security cameras?" I said, sprinting alongside them. "They're gonna see all this."

"Cassie's in Principal Wing's office right now, wiping the security drives," Curtis said.

Kevin grunted and pointed up ahead.

A dark-haired someone huddled behind the water fountain.

Was that—? Could it be? No.

My Kool-Aid king.

My fresh slice of pizza with extra sauce.

My potential but not-quite-yet boyfriend.

"Victor?"

Victor emerged from behind the fountain. *"Hola!"*

"What's he doing here?" Curtis said. Kevin snorted in agreement.

"Sounded like you needed help," Victor said. He proudly held up a walkie-talkie.

Victor winked at me and smiled. I was staring at his dimple so much I almost tripped.

Berna shot me a hard look. "You gave him a walkie?"

"What's everyone mad about?" I said. "Victor's basically a sitter."

"Sitter in Training," Curtis corrected. "He needs to earn his stripes."

Curtis was right. Every babysitter around the world needs to pass Heck Weekend, a grueling two-day exam filled with obstacle courses and monster battles. I pride myself on my good grades, and even I failed it.

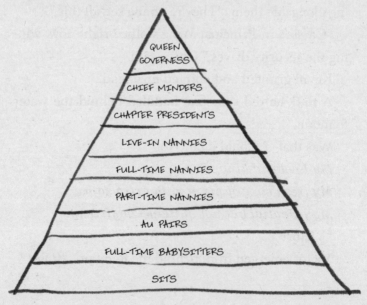

QUEEN
GOVERNESS

CHIEF MINDERS

CHAPTER PRESIDENTS

LIVE-IN NANNIES

FULL-TIME NANNIES

PART-TIME NANNIES

AU PAIRS

FULL-TIME BABYSITTERS

SITS

"I heard something down here!" Principal Wing's voice echoed behind us.

The sound of a mob of faculty members chased after us.

"We have ten seconds before they catch us," Curtis said.

"Less talking more running," Berna said, launching herself down the hall.

We dashed under another banner for the Valentine's Day dance.

"Are you, um, planning on going?" I asked, sprinting beside Victor.

Victor looked at me like I was crazy. "Go to what?"

Curtis slammed into the exit door, but it was rigidly shut.

"Locked? They locked the exits?" Victor asked.

"It *is* a lockdown," I said. "Nothing in or out."

I could hear the teachers charging down the hallway. Our ten-second lead was dwindling fast.

"I knew I should've brought my lock pick to school today," said Curtis.

He whispered into his walkie. "Cassie, this is Curtis. Over."

"Shank you for your ushe of 'over.' Footage ish almosh bleached. Over," replied Cassie.

Curtis squinted up at the remote-controlled

deadbolt. "That's great, Sarge. Think you can override the remote locks? Over."

"Yeah, right. It'sh a middle shkool, not Fort Knosh," Cassie said.

Faculty footsteps thundered toward us. We were trapped.

Kevin aimed his horns directly at the exit and got into a crouching position.

"No!" I knew he could bash it down, but then we'd be left to explain the gaping hole. We needed a smarter, quieter way out. There were no windows in the hall. The only way out I could see was above us.

"Kevin, you're gonna have to lift us up," I said.

"Oooop?" Kevin asked.

"Oooop," I confirmed.

Kevin easily hoisted me to the ceiling. I slid one of the big foam tiles back and grabbed the thin metal rafters. They were shaky, but they held my weight. I crawled inside the small ceiling space as Kevin hoisted up Berna and Curtis.

Victor tried to jump up himself, but he could barely reach.

"Urppa goo!" Kevin said.

Kevin hurled Victor up a little too high, and Victor bumped his head on a rafter. Kevin chuckled. I had a feeling he liked messing with Victor.

"Don't touch any of the tiles," I whispered. "One

false step, and you'll break straight through."

Just before the herd of middle-aged teachers crowded into Hall C, Kevin leaped up beside us and clung to the fire sprinkler pipe. It creaked and threatened to break under his weight. Miraculously, the pipe held. Kevin was the only one who looked amused. Like this was his idea of a fun hang. I carefully slid the foam back into place.

Through a crack in the ceiling tiles, we watched Mr. Milo check the locked exit. Principal Wing hitched up his pants.

"Something that big doesn't just disappear," Principal Wing said.

We clung to the wobbly metal railing, holding our breath. The faculty looked around in defeated confusion and headed back the way they had come. I exhaled. Victor and I exchanged relieved glances.

His big brown eyes sparkled in the dark.

My frizzy red hair fell in my eyes, and I casually flipped it back, trying to look cool. My hair whipped into a dust bunny, and suddenly, I was gagging on a ball of dust. My hand slipped onto a ceiling tile. It broke, like it was made of toast.

I grabbed Victor's shirt, and we both tumbled down to the speckled linoleum in a double thud-crack.

My skull stung. I groaned, blinking through the bubbles bursting in my brain.

"What was that?" Principal Wing said.

A collection of shoe squeaks followed by the sound of a surge of teachers making an about-face behind us.

I saw Kevin and Berna and Curtis watching us from their hiding place in the ceiling.

"Hide, you nitwits," I whispered.

A foam ceiling tile slid into place, hiding Kevin's apologetic eyes.

"Victor, are you okay?" I said. "Victor?"

Lying still beside me, Victor was unconscious.

"Victor! Wake up!"

Principal Wing's hand grabbed my shoulder. His sharp nails dug through my sweater and into my skin.

"Help Victor. He's unconscious!" I said.

"Dear Lord, get that boy some water. His neck could be broken," shrieked the principal.

Victor blinked awake and winced in pain. "Where am I?"

"Gosh darn it, Miss Ferguson!" Principal Wing shouted in my face. His blond mustache flared with spittle. "You two are the ones causing all this trouble?"

"Was that you two in my kitchen?" shouted the lunch lady from the middle of the angry crowd.

"Why were you up there? In the ceiling?" demanded the vice principal as he kicked a broken ceiling tile.

"Hiding. Duh," I said.

"Don't you duh me!"

"Take it easy, Carl," Principal Wing said over his shoulder.

"Nobody duhs me!" huffed Vice Principal Flowers. "Duh yourself, girlie." The red veins around his nose turned into an angry purple.

"Thelma, you said a bear was in your kitchen," Principal Wing said, side-eyeing the lunch lady.

A haze of doubt changed the lunch lady's hardened expression. "It was you two who ate all my nuggets?" asked Mrs. Francini.

I took a deep breath. This was really going to sting. But I had to protect Kevin and the other sitters from getting in trouble. There was no point in all of us going down for something so stupid that could jeopardize Kevin and the babysitters.

"Just me," I said, pulling the half-eaten chicken nugget Kevin had given me from my pocket. "Sorry. I was hungry."

Luckily, what they found on me were books, notebooks, a can of Pringles, and a jump rope. PS: in case you're just tuning in, babysitters hide their gear and weapons in toys so parents don't suspect a thing. Perfect for moments like this!

WHAT THEY SAW

Jump Rope

Textbook

HISTORY

Babysitter's Guide

Pencil

Barbie doll

Can of Pringles

WHAT THEY DIDN'T SEE

A giant net for catching goblins

Hiding throwing stars

Don't leave home without it!

Deadly when sharpened

Stun gun

Hiding extendable sitter staff

"*A Babysitter's Guide to Monster Hunting*?" Mr. Milo said, fishing out my notebook.

My neck muscles strained with panic.

"Art project," I said quickly.

The security guard thumbed through the guide's pages of hideous monsters and instructions on how to stop them.

"Whoever heard of a Toadie? Ridiculous," he snorted, slapping the pages shut.

Principal Wing shouted into a bullhorn. "It's okay, everybody. Lockdown's over. Return to your classrooms. Little Miss Culprit and Mr. Ramon have been caught."

Doors to classrooms slowly opened. Faces peered out at me.

The mob of teachers, proud from their capture, marched me to my doom. Instead of torches and pitchforks, they held rulers and pens and bullhorns. I was def not going to the Valentine's Day dance. My mom and dad were going to ground me for life, and I would not be allowed to babysit for a long, long time.

That's when I noticed something odd about the walls in the hallway. They were bare. Every single paper heart had been ripped off. It was as if Valentine's Day had been erased from the school.

5

"I hope you know that this will go down on your permanent record," said Principal Wing.

The rank odor of stale coffee wafted through the administration room leading to the principal's office. The worn-out blue carpet smelled damp. The solid oak door to the principal's office reminded me of a closed coffin lid.

"There's a lot of factors to this—" I tried.

"There is one excuse for stupid and that's stupid, as my grandmother used to say."

"Well, I think I deserve—"

"You don't deserve a thing. You and that Victor friend of yours are in a heap load of trouble."

"He didn't do anything. It's my fault."

"His parents are immigrants, you know."

"Whoa. What's that got to do with it?"

"Don't whoa me, young lady. They worked very hard to get into this country, and now you're going to destroy their son's future so you can get your kicks? I won't have it, young miss. I will not. One. Week. Suspension," Mr. Wing said.

My heart weighed a ton. I was a straight-A student. Suspension was not my thing.

"Please. I'm one of the few kids here who actually likes going to school," I said.

"Which is why this is all so confusing to me, Kelly," he said.

And then to make things perfectly lemon-in-a-paper-cut awful, Principal Wing called my mother and demanded she leave work and pick up her no-good, delinquent daughter.

Outside the window the cold February wind whirled through bony branches. A crow perched on a tree and blinked at me.

"Go straight to your locker," said Principal Wing, combing his mustache.

"Yes, sir," I said. But as soon as I turned the corner, I ducked into the school clinic to pay Victor a visit. He was lying down, holding an ice pack to his head.

I covered my mouth. My throat tightened. Tears welled. "I'm so sorry," I said.

35

"It's okay," he said, woozy. "Babysitters for life, right?"

"Babysitters for life," I said.

"Kelly. I have to ask you . . . ," he said.

"Save your strength," I whispered.

"It's about the dance."

"Speak up, darling. I can't hear you."

The white curtain was flung back. "You can't be in here!" yelled the nurse.

"One second," I said.

"He needs to rest before his parents come and pick him up. Out!"

"He's in the middle of a sentence," I insisted.

Victor gave me a watery smile and closed his eyes.

"Kelly."

I leaned close to hear him say softly, "Kelly Ferguson."

I walked back to my locker, slumped with uncertainty.

Was he going to ask me to the dance, or was he delirious?

At my locker, Berna, Cassie, and Curtis quietly gathered around me. Their friendship felt like a force field.

"At least we got Kevin out," Berna said.

I tried to open my locker, but it was stuck. "Victor's hurt."

"Nish guy, but I worry about him. Little nervoush in the shervishe," said Cassie.

"Give him a chance, Cassie," Berna said. "You kept tripping over your shoelaces when you first started."

"They were too long for my shoe shize," Cassie growled.

"Why couldn't Kevin show us his drawing after school?" Berna asked. "Why did he have to come all the way here to talk to you, Kelly?"

I angrily forced open my locker.

A flood of cut-out hearts spilled from my locker in a wave of crimson construction paper. All the hearts from the hallway had been stuffed inside.

"Oooooh. Now I get it," Berna said.

Curtis and Cassie giggled, standing ankle-deep in Valentine's Day art.

"Monster Boy's got a crush you," Berna said.

"What did we agree on, Kelly?" my mother shouted, driving me away from school. "You can hunt your monsters and babysit and fight the forces of evil, but you need to stay in school and keep your grades up. That was the deal, was it not?"

She punctuated that last sentence by banging her hand against the steering wheel.

"Yes," I said, hanging my head. "It was."

After the events of the Spider Queen invasion this past Christmas, I told my parents the truth: I'm a monster-hunting babysitter. They took the news surprisingly well. Especially when they learned that I was the one who saved their lives. Points for that. They sat down with the Rhode Island chapter president, Mama

Vee, who talked them through the job and told them that I had killed not one but two of the seven Boogeypeople. Mama Vee was once my babysitter, and my parents still trusted her opinion after all these years. I think it gave my folks a sense of pride that I was protecting kids.

Then I showed them how I handled a Bushido blade, and my mom actually gave me a standing ovation. Who knew she loved swordplay so much?

My dad just sat on the couch and said "wow" the whole time.

So we cut a deal. I could still hunt monsters as long as it didn't affect my schoolwork. And I had to promise to always text and let them know I was okay. It was not easy, slaying and studying as hard as I did. But I did it.

"Given the circumstances, I would say your father and I have been rather understanding of your new lifestyle, wouldn't you?"

"I would say yes."

"I think I'm doing an excellent job of giving you your space. Your father's a nervous wreck, but I told him you needed room to blossom and grow and find your own path."

"And I appreciate that."

"But when I have to leave work, to beg Mrs. Zellman, my boss, the mother of the boy who was abducted by some Boogeyman under your watch—"

"I got him back," I added.

"Not the point! I cannot ask my boss to give me two hours so I can pick up my delinquent daughter from her school because she's been suspended."

"I didn't mean to," I said. "And I am so sorry."

My mother shook her head in utter bewilderment. "Who eats three hundred chicken nuggets? Is there something wrong with you? Do you have a parasite in your stomach?"

"No."

"Do you have an eating disorder?"

"No."

"That is coming out of your babysitting fund, believe me. You need to learn the value of a dollar because your father and I cannot afford to flush money down the toilet."

"Mom! I didn't eat the nuggets." I said, throwing up my hands. "It was Kevin!"

My mom knew all about Kevin. Except for the part where he maybe had a crush on me.

As we pulled into the driveway, my mother shook her head. "That poor, poor boy. Has anyone found a cure for him?"

"He likes being what he is," I said with a shrug. "He's pretty cool when he's not causing trouble."

"He must be very lonely," my mother said. "It's good that you're his friend. But that doesn't change the fact that you're grounded for the week of your suspension."

She parked. I didn't get out. The seat belt twisted in my tightening grip. I was really going to have to thread the needle on this one.

"So, Mom, the Valentine's Day dance is in five days, and, look, I totally get that I'm grounded, but . . ." The seat belt groaned in my fist. "I may or may not be going with Victor and . . ."

"You should have thought of that before you got yourself suspended."

She turned off the car and headed into the house. I felt the wind get knocked out of me.

"Wait, Mom, please! This is the *Valentine's Day* dance." I followed after her. "It wasn't even my fault. It was Kevin! I—"

"You want to be this big grown-up girl who slays dragons and whatnot, then you need to take more responsibility for your actions and understand they have consequences," she said, unlocking the front door. "Don't blame monsters for your problems."

After we shook off our coats inside, Mom held out her hand. I stared at it.

"Phone," she said.

"Can I give you my kidney instead?" I pleaded.

"Hand it over. And I want to see homework. And chores. Laundry. Studying. De-icing the driveway."

My jaw dropped. This was a new level of cruelty.

"I saved you from the Spider Queen," I said.

"And I'm forever grateful, but you messed up big-time. Phone."

I exhaled the heaviest of breaths, locked eyes with the woman who claimed to love me, and handed her my entire electric life. She slid my phone into her purse. I flopped dramatically onto the couch.

"I have to babysit for the Renfield twins tonight," I muttered to the ceiling.

"You'll just have to cancel."

"I can't cancel. That's unprofessional."

"That Liz girl does it to you all the time."

"I'm not Liz. And the Renfields booked this appointment a month ago, Mom. It's their anniversary or something. Canceling a few hours before a job makes me look flakey."

My mother pinched the bridge of her nose.

"Why couldn't you have taken up piano or soccer? Why did it have to be babysitting? I'd like to see the kitchen windows cleaned by the time I'm back from work at seven." My mom grabbed her bag to head back to her office. "Good-bye."

It was only one thirty. Normally, I would be in American history. Instead, I was strolling through my house feeling an odd, guilt-ridden freedom.

My house phone was huge and plastic and nailed to the wall. Its twisted, sinewy cord tugged when I took it from the cradle. The giant buttons clicked with each number I entered. So what if I knew Victor's number by heart backward and forward?

"Victor, hi!" I said trying to sound chipper. "Are you okay? I'm so, so, sorry. How's your head?"

"*¿Quien es esto?*" I cringed. His dad had answered Victor's phone. I could hear Victor's mom crying in the background. "Kelly F?"

"*Hola, padre de* Victor. It's me, Kelly Ferguson! *Amiga de* Victor. *¿Cómo está* Victor?*"

"My son could have broken his head because of you," said Victor's father. His voice was low and grim.

Oh no, no. His family hates me!

"I'm so sorry. I feel so bad, sir," I said. "Is there anything I can do?"

"You can stay away from my son."

My stomach wrenched.

"You have brought pain and suffering to our family!" Victor's mother wailed in the background.

"Our family cannot make waves. Not now. This is our home. You understand? I will not have you endanger my family."

And then there was silence. His father had hung up on me.

I swallowed the lump in my throat.

"Let the punishment begin," I sighed.

I did a little math homework. I read about the Battle of the *Monitor* and the *Merrimack* during the Civil War in my American history textbook. I chilled on the couch and pretended to check Instagram on my invisible phone. I read a chapter of *Little Women* for English class.

"'For love casts out fear, and gratitude can conquer pride,'" I said, reading aloud to no one.

Homework finally done, I took my framed special edition *Beauty and the Beast* movie poster off my bedroom wall and stared at the collection of Kevin's drawings. There were lots of sketches of rides and roller coasters, and a huge dark pit filled with glimmering eyes. Kevin had even managed to draw us a rough map of Monster Island.

I taped Kevin's latest master piece of the ELL building to the wall and stood back to take it all in. It looked terrifying.

I opened my babysitter's guide to a new page and wrote down everything we knew.

NAME: Monster Island

LOCATION: Unknown (thanks to Kevin LeRue, we know it's somewhere off the coast of Maine)

ORIGIN: The island's existence has been known but never found

INHABITANTS: Baron Von Eisenvult (aka Boogeyperson #7), sea snakes, gremlins, man-eating fauna

TERRAIN: Not much is known. Treacherous. Heavy forestation.

BUILDINGS: Unknown (thanks to Kevin LeRue, we know a few more things)—Professor Gonzalo's laboratory (Gonzalo, the fifth Boogeyman, is working for the Baron). This is where kids are transformed into monsters. For details of the laboratory see Kevin's drawings. According to Kevin there is a mine/rock quarry where imprisoned monster kids dig for . . . diamonds? Gold? Unknown. There is a small prison/stables where the monster kids are kept.

Under the Buildings section of the guide, I carefully wrote: "Ell" building en Route to island?

As the Boogeypeople's prisoner, Kevin was allowed to see very little of the island, and there were a lot of gaps in his maps. His only memory of getting to the island was by a boat. He had seen an oil rig through the boat's window, and so we located all the oil rig routes off the New England coast, and that narrowed down our search area to fifty possible sections.

I brought my handbook to our family computer in the hallway.

Hey, Mom didn't say I couldn't Google stuff about mysterious monster islands while I was grounded. This isn't for the likes; this is for the greater good.

"ELL." There were millions of possibilities.

"ELL" could have been the middle of a word, the beginning of it, or the end.

I called my smartest, fastest friend. It took me a few times to remember her number.

"Hello? Who is this?" Berna said on the other end.

"It's me! Kellymundo. Your valentine," I said.

"Are you calling me from jail?"

"This is my house phone."

"Your what?"

"It's horrible. It smells like my mom's morning breath. Let's not talk about it."

I told her how I thought if we could locate a building

with "ELL" on the side, we might be able to find Monster Island.

Shhh-POP! She blew a bubble into the phone. I could tell when she was thinking hard because her gum chewing grew louder.

"Bell Labs for Disease Control," Berna said. "It's the only thing I can find that fits within our search parameters." I looked up Bell Labs, and as always, Berna was right.

There was an island with a Bell Labs for Disease Control on it off the coast of Maine.

"Looks like they're a private chemical company that specializes in disease control."

"Like they make diseases? Gross," I said.

"More like they store them and test them. Wow. They have everything at Bell Labs. Chicken pox. Mumps. Purple Bulinga. The bubonic plague."

"Yikes."

I scrolled through sites about Bell Labs. There were all sorts of kooky conspiracy theories about the place. Nutty people thought Bell Labs was hired by the government to create a superflu to wipe out all humankind in the name of population control. Other conspiracy theorists claimed Bell Labs was testing humans and building creatures. People on a nearby island said a hideous being that had washed up on their shores had been created in the Bell Labs. On one conspiracy site there was a photograph of the building taken from a boat. It matched Kevin's drawing.

On the map I tracked where the Bell Labs was located and saw the only piece of land close to it was a small, remote speck in the middle of nowhere.

"What about this place? Sunshine Island?" I asked.

"The only info I can find about it says it's remote and uninhabited." I could hear Berna clacking away on her keyboard at lightning speed. "With the exception of a few shipwrecks in the surrounding waters, Sunshine Island is a forgotten crumb unworthy of mention. A nowhere place that no one has ever visited."

"Sunshine Island," I said. "It's the perfect hiding place."

Shhh-POP! Berna sharply snapped a bubble in agreement.

"It would explain all the weird stuff happening near Bell Labs," she said.

"Like, what if the monsters washing up on the shores near Bell Labs are actually coming from Sunshine Island?" I said.

"Bingo," she said.

The small spot on Kevin's map was the shape of an upside-down heart, adrift in the endless sea. Something tightened in my chest. Had we finally found the island where Kevin and so many other kids had been taken and imprisoned by monsters? Was this really the home of the Baron, the deadliest Boogeyperson on the planet? And was I really going to risk my life to go there to rescue a bunch of kids I didn't even know?

An answer to these questions arose that made my insides shudder.

That answer was a determined yes.

My dad got home from work, brushed the grease off his nails, and chugged a soda.

"Let's go, kiddo!" He grabbed his keys and waved warily for me to follow him. "I talked with your mother. You can look after these kids tonight, Kells, but after that no more for a while."

"Yes. You're the best."

"I know," he grumbled as we got into his car.

On the way to my babysitting job, it was his turn to lecture me about responsibility, thinking clearly, and the importance of getting a good education. But he didn't sound angry. Ever since he found out I hunt monsters I think he's been a little scared of me.

Is it bad that I'm okay with that?

"Yes, Dad," I said. "You're so right."

My overly nice voice made me cringe. I was playing the sad-but-sweet-daughter card. If I could get my dad on my side, maybe he could get my mom to lighten my sentence.

"I appreciate you not screaming at me," I said, pretending to get choked up. "Victor's parents yelled at me earlier."

"Victor's parents did what?" A vein in his neck popped. "No one yells at my kid but me."

We drove across the giant Newport Pell Bridge. Far down below, February winds raked the waves white.

Beyond the sparse main street shops of Jamestown, we passed a real working windmill and then turned onto a long, empty street. The house where I would be babysitting stood out against the sky with pristine pride. It looked like a giant, two-story dollhouse with a gingerbread roof. It was the cleanest, neatest house I had ever seen. And it totally gave me the creeps. I studied the sculpted thickets in the front yard for any lurking ghouls.

"Are there going to be, y'know, things here?" my dad said.

"Hasn't been much activity for the past few weeks," I said, trying to sound like all this monster hunting and sitting was no big deal. "No need to worry, Dad."

"I'm your pop. I worry. It's my job." He grabbed my shoulder and locked eyes with me. "If any creepers come round, you call me or your mother or the police," he said.

"Mom took my phone away," I said.

He flipped me my phone.

I caught it. My phone!

"For emergencies only," he said.

I yelped gratefully and kissed him on the cheek.

"If one of those whatevers pops up, you call me, I got something for them in the trunk. I'm your father. I'll whup any six-eyed sloth thing—"

"Sleeknatch, Dad," I gently corrected.

"Right. Whatever. Anything like that, you call me and I'll come. No questions. I got your back. I mean it. I'm right around the corner. Meeting a buddy for a beer five minutes away."

"Dad!"

"What? He lives in the area."

"You can't spy on me."

"I'm seeing a friend."

"You don't have any friends."

"I've got you. You're my friend."

"Love you, Dad."

"No apps or face-chats or whatever. I'll be back at ten o'clock," he called after me as I darted up the red brick pathway. "It's a school night."

"I don't have school tomorrow, remember?" I said over my shoulder.

"That's not a good thing! Don't push your luck."

"Could be later. Depends on the parents, Dad!"

"I don't care. I'll be here at ten either way."

His car clunked down the street, leaving an icy trail of exhaust. I pressed the power button on my phone.

"Dang it!" I said.

The battery was dead.

"Rawk! Rawk!"

A crow hopped on the walkway in front of me, watching me with cold, dark curiosity. I flapped my arm, but it didn't move. I had to walk around it on my way to the front door.

"Get away, goth chicken," I said.

There was a metal creak from the middle of the door.

Two eyes peered up at me through the brass mail slot.

"Hi! It's Kelly. Your babysitter!"

The eyes seemed to smile up at me.

The tiny brass door snapped shut. A series of locks click-clacked on the other side of the large door until it creaked open. In a burst of wings, the crow flew off behind me.

At the door stood a seven-year-old girl, one of the Renfield twins. She was wearing a neat red dress with a large ladybug sewn on the front, a white turtleneck, white leggings, and blue shoes with buckles on them. Her hair was braided perfectly into the shape of a large tight bow.

I bit my lip, wondering which twin she was . . . *Ursula or Sabina?*

I had babysat the Renfield sisters twice before. They were cute and they had great manners, and their outfits were always perfectly matched. It was hard to tell them apart, but I knew that Ursula was the shy one, and Sabina was the chatty one.

"Hi, Sabina," I said, I taking off my puffy jacket.

She smiled. Phew! I relaxed.

"We've been expecting you!" said Sabina.

She gently stroked the hair of a doll in her arm.

"I like your dress," I said.

Sabina smiled coyly. "Thank you. I made it myself."

"Are you sure your mom didn't help?" I asked playfully.

Sabina scowled and thrust her doll in my face.

"Look, lady," Sabina said in her high-pitched dolly voice, "if Sabina says she made it herself, she made it herself."

I was not going to start the night off arguing with a sarcastic doll. Especially an expensive Fancy Lady doll.

"Say hi to Lilly May," Sabina demanded.

"Hi, Lilly May."

Sabina loved Lilly May. She'd met ("met" not "bought") her little plastic pal at the Fancy Lady Doll Store, where they sell Fancy Lady doll clothes and Fancy Lady doll jewelry and Fancy Lady doll purses. There is even a Fancy Lady stable of horses if you're into that kind of thing. Sabina's doll's outfit looked like it cost more than mine.

I checked the living room. For a house with two kids in it, it was remarkably clean. Nothing was out of place. I felt like I was standing in a furniture catalog. But . . .

Where was the clatter of parents getting ready for their night out?

"Where's your mom, Sabina?"

Sabina shook her fancy doll and continued to speak in her screechy voice. "They left five minutes ago because you were late."

"They left you here alone?" I said.

"That's what I said," Sabina snapped in her doll voice.

"Lilly May, be nice," Sabina said apologetically.

The mean doll voice was a new thing with Sabina, and it was already getting on my nerves. If she was going to use her doll to insult me but pretend like she was sorry, we were going to have problems.

"They left a note," Sabina said, pointing.

A typed letter was attached to the refrigerator by a sun-shaped magnet.

We had to leave early. We will
be home soon. Have fun.
The girls' new bedtime is midnight.

The Parents of Sabina and Ursula.

I glanced at the paper. I knew the girls' parents liked things neat and tidy, but this was a little suspicious.

I peeked at the innocent-looking child before me.

"Sabina, if you're going to fake a letter from your parents, you're gonna have to do better than this."

Sabina looked shocked. "Why would I do that, Kelly?"

"Because you want to stay up until midnight."

"My bedtime is eight p.m. You know that, silly billy."

"Sabina, where's your sister?"

Sabina smirked, as if she had been waiting for me to ask that question. "Somewhere."

"Where?" I said with increasing concern.

She waved the doll, making its long, flowing hair flap back and forth against its fleshy rubber face.

"Hide-and-seek!" she shrieked in her doll voice. Sabina giggled and darted down the hallway.

9

This was getting bizarre. I didn't want to play this strange game of theirs. I whipped a charger from my backpack and plugged my phone into the kitchen wall. An urgent need to call the twins' parents came over me, but I had to wait for my phone battery to charge. Plus, I didn't know their phone numbers like I knew Victor's and Berna's.

I tightened the straps on my backpack and followed Sabina's giggle up a staircase. I found her standing at the end of the hallway, peering at me from around the corner.

"Sabina, where's your sister?" I said.

The little girl snickered. "Silly. I'm Ursula."

"Very funny, Sabina."

"I'm Ursula!" the little girl screamed, and stomped her foot.

Sabina or Ursula or whoever ducked around the corner. The twin games had begun.

"Hide-and-seek already?" I called out. "I'm a master at this. You got three minutes, tops."

The house was larger than I remembered, and I found myself standing in another long corridor. The twins were poised at the end of the hall, perfectly still, each with the same tiny smiles on their faces. My heart pounded as I inched closer.

Just a giant, creepy photograph. Phew!

I flung open door number one. It was a pristine bathroom with all-white tiles. The shower curtain was drawn closed. I whisked it back. *Shink!* The tub was empty.

Thump, thump, thump.

Tiny footsteps darted above me. The light fixture hanging from the ceiling bounced and clinked.

Thump, thump, thump.

I gulped.

Are they on the roof?

"Hey, you guys!" I shouted up at them. "You can't be up there! Enough already."

The tiny footsteps stopped.

I was about to climb out of a window and scale my way to the roof when I spotted a cord dangling from the ceiling in the hall. The trap door to the attic.

The springs twanged as I pulled the rope. *Snap!* The ladder flipped open like a switchblade. I barely missed getting my teeth bashed in.

The flimsy ladder squeaked under my steps. I carefully poked my head up into the attic. It smelled like a hamster cage up there. Boxes and unwanted things were piled to the ceiling and covered with sheets.

"You're getting warmer" Sabina's voice echoed.

"I really don't think we should be playing up here," I said. "I fell out of a ceiling this morning. It is no fun. Believe me."

Boards crisscrossed the floor over pink puffs of insulation and frayed wires. Moonlight poured in through the two oval windows, illuminating a picnic blanket.

A dozen dolls were seated on the blanket, circling a plastic tea set. Some were Fancy Lady dolls; some were antique and porcelain-faced. Tiny teacups had been placed in front of them.

One of the sheets rose suddenly and walked toward me. I whooshed it from Sabina's head, and she burst into a fit of hysterical laugher.

"I scared you! I scared you!" she screamed, and pointed up at me.

"Takes more than that to scare a babysitter," I said.

I caught a glimpse of movement in a dusty mirror.

Ursula was crouched behind a box, holding her knees to her chest. Her long, wavy hair hung over her face.

"The winner and still Hide-and-Seek world champion," I said, raising my fists in the air.

"I wasn't hiding," said Ursula from under her curtain of hair. "I was making tea."

There were dark rings under Ursula's eyes. Her fingernails were dirty. I noticed a broken piece of twig tangled in her hair. I reached for it, but she pulled away.

"Come play with us," Ursula said.

Ursula sank close beside Sabina in the circle of dolls and poured invisible tea.

"Why don't we have your little tea party downstairs where it's safer," I suggested.

Ursula shook her head and whispered, "They like it better up here."

"Fix your hair, Ursula. This is a formal gathering," Sabina shrieked in her doll voice.

Ursula pulled her messy hair back into a ponytail.

"Hey, be nice," I said to Sabina.

"That wasn't me. That was Lilly May," Sabina said innocently.

I glared at the blank-faced doll. "Be nice, Lilly May," I said. "Or I'll put you in time-out."

Sabina and Ursula exchanged worried glances.

"You shouldn't talk to her like that," Ursula mumbled.

"Well, your sister can't talk to you like that either," I said sternly.

61

They passed a secret between their eyes.

"I'm sorry, sister," said Sabina.

"That's better," I said. "Now can we please take this party to the living room? It's freezing up here, and there's like a million health and safety hazards waiting to happen."

I held out my hand for Ursula. Don't think I didn't notice that the twins looked to Lilly May for an answer.

"We'll go after our song," said Sabina.

"Yes! Our song!" said Ursula.

Sabina held her hand out to me. "Hold my hand, Kelly," said Sabina.

A shaft of starlight beamed down on us as we linked hands in the cold attic.

"Now let us begin," Sabina said.

The whites of her eyes grew larger as they began to sing.

"We're the best of friends we ever could be! The best, best the world will ever see!
Watch us sparkle! Watch us sing! We're the Fancy Lady dolls, and we're everything!
We're your best friends, and we're everything, everything, EVERYTHING!"

I frowned. Just when I thought the twins were going to bust out into a seance, they were singing the commercial for the Fancy Lady doll company. Kids these days. *"Forever and ever, Fancy Lady dolls, we are everything!"* the twins rejoiced.

They gave themselves a big round of applause.

"Did you like that, Lilly May?" Ursula said.

"Yes, Lilly May, did you like it?" Sabina asked.

The doll stared lifelessly ahead.

Something is definitely up. Last time I was here, they were not this odd. The only thing different is Lilly May. I need to get that doll away from these girls and inspect it pronto.

A figment of a memory from *A Babysitter's Guide to Monster Hunting* flashed into my brain.

NAME: Dolls (for creepy puppets, see Pinocchio; murderous ventriloquist dummies, flip to V; for Demonic Toys, see Tiki Terrors)

HEIGHT: 1'-2'

WEIGHT: 1/2-1 lbs, depending on material it's made of

TYPE: Class 4 (dolls are pretty fragile and can easily be done in with a lawn mower or even a weed whacker)

LIKES: Tea parties. Dresses. Pretty, shiny things like kitchen knives

DISLIKES: Lawn mowers, ugly people. Being told no.

WEAKNESSES: Lawn mowers, microwaves. Being gift wrapped.

STRENGTHS: Supercute. Crafty. Knife work. Cunning. Small size makes them good with sneak attacks. And this point cannot be stressed enough: they are really good with knives.

ORIGIN: Dolls can come alive for various reasons. They may be possessed by the spirit of a bad person who was murdered and needed a quick body to inhabit and is now angry to be stuck in a tiny plastic frame. The doll itself could

be animated by a spell, or there could
be a confused demon inside the doll.

On rare occasions they may be humans who
have been eerily reduced in size and enjoy
wearing tiny, fancy clothes.

ASSESSMENT: Little girls can have a profound
connection with their dolls. Beware their
influence. If the living doll turns out to be a
nice little buddy, no sweat. Leave it alone. Sure,
it's weird, but kids can handle it. But if it's
an evil doll, arm yourself and build a big fire in
the fireplace.

**DO NOT try to take the doll away from the
child. Instead, offer a trade in exchange for
the doll.

Good luck because once a kid loves her doll
she will want to be with it forever.

While Ursula poured Sabina more invisible tea, I
studied Lilly May. The dark-eyed toy seemed to stare
back at me. Lilly May had a plastic smile and a casual
coolness to her expression that made her look like nothing in the world could bother her. Her happy-dead eyes
beamed away. Lilly May the doll had it all figured out.

You've gone nuts, Kelly. You've entered a staring contest with an inanimate object purchased at the mall.

I clapped my hands together. "Okay! How 'bout we go downstairs, and I'll make everyone some hot cocoa!"

"Yay!" said Ursula, jumping to her feet. "With extra marshmallows!"

Sabina glared at her sister. Ursula stopped.

Sabina slowly stood up and took Lilly May with her as I led them carefully across the boards toward the rickety ladder. I peered down at the carpeted floor below.

"I'll go first and help you guys—"

Tiny hands shoved into my back and ushered me forward.

The world spun as I tumbled down the ladder.

CRACK! THUD!

The floor smacked me in the face. My vision snapped into darkness.

The ceiling blurred above me as I awoke to the twins dragging me down the hall by my arms.

"Ursula, come on. I'm doing all the work here," Sabina snapped at her sister.

"I'm trying. She's heavy," Ursula whined. "And her backpack keeps catching on stuff."

In one swift move (the Folding and Flying Diaper, page 227, illustration 4A, from the guide) I yanked my arms down, sending the little girls tumbling to the floor while I used their momentum to spring to my feet. I stood over them.

"It wasn't us," cried Ursula. "It was Lilly May!"

"Be quiet, Ursula!" snapped Sabina in a shaky voice. "It was you. Tell the truth!"

"Stop lying!" screamed Ursula. "You're scared what Lilly May will do to you."

My head throbbed in pain. I squinted through my headache.

"Stop screeching," I said, rubbing my sore face. "I'm calling your parents. I don't know which one of you did it, but you cannot push people like that. You're lucky I know how to crash-land or I could have broken my neck. Both of you are in big trouble."

Sabina's lower lip trembled. I shook my head, preparing myself for the onslaught of tears.

"She did it," Sabina whispered.

I looked at Ursula.

"Not her," Sabina whispered again. "Lilly May."

Her eyes were big and pleading. She was begging me to believe her.

A non-babysitter type person would have accused her of telling a fib, but not me. It was my job to listen to the weird and the bizarre tales kids told.

Lilly May was not in Sabina's arms. I peered up at the attic, expecting to see the doll giggling down at me. The attic was still. The hairs on the back of my neck electrified.

"Where's Lilly May now?" I murmured.

The twins sniffed and wiped their noses.

"You believe us?" Sabina said in wonder.

"Of course I believe you."

"She told us we had to," said Ursula.

"Lilly May hates babysitters," said Sabina.

"She said it was the only way."

A metallic clang echoed through the house. It came from the kitchen.

"Go to your room right now," I said. "Lock the door and wait for me to say it's safe."

"Please don't go down there, Miss Kelly," Sabina said. "She's mean."

"Don't worry, kid. I'm a babysitter. We eat killer dolls for breakfast."

They ran off to their room and slammed the door.

Click-clack! My bo-staff snapped into place as I stalked down the stairs. Peering into the kitchen I saw one of the drawers had been pulled opened. Knives were spilled across the kitchen floor.

Why couldn't it have been spoons? Spoons aren't scary at all.

I gripped my staff tight and scanned the area.

A tuft of hair poked out from behind the garbage can in the corner. I crouched into Baby Panther position to keep my footsteps quiet as I approached the killer doll. I jabbed my staff behind the garbage can and pinned her to the ground.

"Got you!"

Immediately, I knew I had made a terrible mistake. The doll was not Lilly May. It was a Raggedy Ann. A decoy. Behind me a cabinet door flew open. In a burst of cornflakes, Lilly May dove at me, swinging a huge butcher knife. I spun and batted her across the kitchen, like I was hitting a home run. The little doll bounced into the refrigerator.

Her pretty face snarled at me. The knife wavered in her tiny grip.

"This is my house now, babysitter," Lilly May shrieked. Her voice sounded like Sabina's creepy doll voice. "Those girls belong to me."

"Not on my watch, doll," I said, getting into warrior stance.

Lilly May skittered toward me crazy fast, blade raised over her head. I stepped back and bumped into the pantry. I was not expecting her to be so quick. She hacked wildly at my ankles, but I managed to block her with my staff.

I flipped her like a pancake, and she flew across the kitchen, but this time she sprang off the refrigerator and came hurling back at me like a bullet. I ducked, and her knife stabbed the wall. She dangled from the handle. Her little legs kicked furiously.

Lilly May let out a chilling battle cry and launched at my face. I blocked her with my staff, but she grabbed on to it, and her little Mary Janes kicked me in the chin, rapid-fire.

Thwack! Lilly May snapped my own staff in my face.

Ow! *Get a grip, Kelly. You're getting beat up by a doll!*

I blinked through the buzzing pain in my nose. Lilly May hopped down and reached for a steak knife. I kicked her and dented in her rubber face. She snapped into whirlwind mode, flinging knives at me.

The staff isn't helping. Adapt, Kelly. Go in for close combat.

I tossed the staff. Grabbed a knife. *Clang!*

The evil doll and I crossed blades.

"You're good," I said, huffing for breath. "Who made you?"

Lilly May sneered, turned around, and showed me her butt.

"Made in China" was stamped into her right cheek.

"That's where I was made. Where I was *born* is another story," she said.

I bumped into the oven. I tripped. Dropped my knife.

"You win," I said, holding up my hands. "Please don't hurt me."

A warped smile spread across Lilly May's pushed-in face.

"I'm not going to hurt you, babysitter. I'm just going to kill you!"

She lunged. I spun and opened the oven door. The doll roared inside. I slammed it shut.

Pressing my shoulder against it, I cranked the heat knobs up to five hundred degrees.

"Let me out!" screamed the doll. She banged her rubber fists against the glass.

"What's the matter? Can't take the heat?" I said.

The temperature gauge rose past a hundred.

"If I were you, I'd start answering my questions."

Through the dark glass, I could see Lilly May's panicked face as she watched the tips of her fingers melt like candle wax.

"What do you want with the twins?" I demanded.

"They're naughty. And naughty children get what they deserve," she hissed. "A special treat. Someplace fun."

"Sunshine Island?" I blurted out.

The temperature rose to two hundred. Lilly May started to do a little marching dance as she began to sing.

"There's a place the lucky children go,
Where fun is forever and you never get old.
A land of cupcakes and ice cream.
Rides and slides to make you scream."

Lilly May's face started to sag and droop. Her voice was getting lower and lower.

72

"Adventure, toys, and so much fun.
Follow me to the land of sun."

A huge heat bubble grew to the size of a peach on Lilly May's rubber neck. Her hands smeared against the hot glass.

"Let me out, you monster!" she wailed until her jaw oozed down the front of her dress.

Plastic eyeballs lazily fell from their sockets as her head collapsed onto her shoulders, and the wicked toy melted into a slimy mess.

Coughing, I waved the black smoke away to see the Fancy Lady doll was now a pile of smoldering clothes and a charred black puddle.

The smoke alarm screeched. I opened a window and waved the smoke out. I grabbed a dustpan and scraped the burned remains into the trash can.

Two tiny screams rang behind me.

The twins stood in the kitchen doorway, watching me scoop up their doll's remains.

"Lilly May!" cried Sabina and Ursula.

"I'm fine, thanks for asking," I said. "Don't touch the knives."

Raw pain bit my arm. I had been cut a few times. I pulled a small first aid kit from my bag. The twins stared at me from across the countertop.

73

Sabina shook her head sadly. "You didn't have to fry her."

"Never was a good cook," I said.

Sabina scowled at me. Her right shoulder was slumped, as if part of her had been severed. She rubbed her forehead, wincing.

"You okay?" I asked. "Got a headache?"

"No," she snapped. "I'm fine."

"Where did you get that doll?" I said, cleaning my wounds.

"She was nice when we met her at the mall. But then she got weird," Ursula said. "Daddy accidentally ran her over with a snowblower."

"Lilly May lost an arm. So we took her to the doll hospital. Three days ago."

"The nice doctor lady there fixed her up. But when Lilly May came home, she started talking. For real."

Sabina smiled. No regrets. "She was fun. She was our secret."

"Lilly May was mean," said Ursula.

"She wanted to take us somewhere fun, Ursula! Sunshine Island sounds amazing. Like better than any park in the world," said Sabina.

My stomach sank. "When was Lilly May going to take you there?" I asked.

"Tonight," Sabina said, and nodded at the trash can.

"But we'll never get to go to the most amazingest place in the world now because you melted my best friend."

Sabina burst into a flood of very dramatic sobs.

"Where's this doll hospital?" I asked.

"Mommy and Daddy would know. They didn't like Lilly May," Ursula whispered.

"And she didn't like Mommy and Daddy," Sabina added, wiping her nose on her sleeve.

They both froze at exactly the same time, as if they had remembered something horrible.

"Mommy and Daddy!"

11

A fluorescent light buzzed in the garage. The twins approached a bulging blue tarp.

"They're going to be so mad," Ursula said.

"Maybe we should leave them alone," Sabina whispered.

I pushed the girls aside and whooshed the tarp off Mrs. and Mr. Renfield. Their wrists were duct-taped together. Their faces were covered in splotchy makeup, as if they had been kidnapped in the middle of playing princess. They weren't breathing.

They were snoring.

"Lilly May slipped a bunch of Mommy's sleeping pills in their water," Sabina said.

"We put them down here," Ursula said. "I gave them a pillow."

"They look so peaceful," said Sabina.

I knelt down and checked their pulses. Heartbeats were regular. I rummaged through my book bag.

"Lilly May put them to sleep so you could run away with her?" I asked.

Sabina nodded. "That was the plan. Until someone came along and melted her."

I studied the girls' dark eyes. Ursula seemed genuinely sorry. Sabina was just sorry she got caught. If the Boogeypeople were looking for naughty children, I could see why they chose Sabina.

"Don't worry," I said. "I can wake them up."

"Do we hafta?" Sabina asked.

In my backpack I found a small case full of ingredients I had gathered from different monsters, each numbered and Velcro'ed in place.

I hadn't quite mastered babysitter chemistry yet, but I knew a few mixtures.

One part stink beetle, three parts hobgoblin warts, and a moldy one-eyed sloth's toenail.

"Untie them," I said.

"Do we hafta?" Sabina repeated.

"Yes, we hafta!" I snapped.

The twins undid their parents' bonds while I shook

the concoction together and waved the pungent yellow smoke under the Renfields' noses. They sputtered awake and looked around in total shock.

They had a million questions. "Why are we asleep in the garage? Was that doll really trying to kill us?"

I did my best to explain.

Usually, we sitters keep mum about monsters, but in this instance, I thought the Renfields should know that something was up with their adorable twins in case the girls tried to make a break for Sunshine Island again.

Also, I wanted to clock out before my dad came to pick me up so I could investigate the doll hospital. It was only eight o'clock. That gave me two hours to figure this all out.

Mrs. Renfield's trembling hands found a receipt for the doll hospital in her purse. The address was on its letterhead.

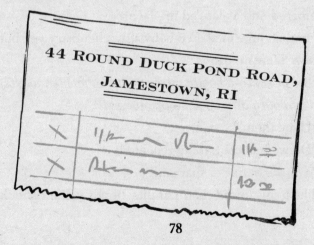

44 ROUND DUCK POND ROAD, JAMESTOWN, RI

I excused myself and called for backup.

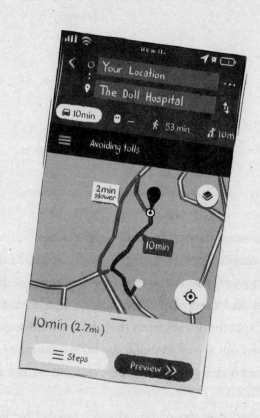

12

"Makes sense to me," said Liz LeRue as the babysitter mobile sped toward the doll hospital. "Lure kids to an awesome island with the promise of fun and games and then turn them into a monster army. Instead of snatching kids from their beds, the Boogeys have figured out a way to make the little ones come to them—with no delivery fees. Like Amazon Prime for monsters."

Liz rubbed the top of her shaved head. She had recently buzzed off all her hair, which made her look tougher and meaner than her usual fifteen-year-old self. Her look scared a lot of parents, but I knew Liz wouldn't really stomp anyone's teeth in—without a reason.

Liz drove the sitter mobile, a beat-up van that had been shredded and bashed but miraculously still ran. I was buckled up in the passenger seat. Kevin was stinking up the back seat. Our hobgoblin buddy and brilliant mechanic, Wugnot, had outfitted the van with a bubble window on the roof, which fit Kevin's horns comfortably.

"I tried getting Berna and the others to come, but they were already on other jobs," said Liz. "Not that we need 'em with me and big Kev. Right, Kev?"

Kevin and Liz howled together.

"We're investigating," I said. "We can't make a bunch of noise."

"Oh, I beg your pardon, princess," Liz said with a smirk. "Who do you think you're talking to?" She pointed to herself and then to her beastly brother. "We're the pros from Pawtucket. And don't you faw-get it."

Kevin barked in agreement. I shot him a look.

"If you're such a pro, why did you get me suspended from school today?"

Kevin made apologetic grunts.

"Toughen up, newb," Liz said. "I've been suspended dozens of times."

"Victor got a concussion, too," I said.

Keven could barely contain his laughter.

"It's not funny, Kevin. He got hurt. I don't like my friends getting hurt. Not him. Not you."

Liz snorted. "How does Victor think he can be a babysitter if he freaks out around monsters when he's not even on a job?"

"It was my fault," I said.

"Kev said he choked," Liz said.

"Kevin!" I shouted.

Kevin guffawed.

"Victor's going to be a great babysitter. You'll see."

"You're only saying that because he's your boyfriend and you love him," Liz said.

Kevin looked at me with puppy dog eyes. "Urv?" he yelped.

"Urv is a big word, Kev," I sighed.

"What do you know about love and romance, Liz?" I asked.

"Nothing. Gladly. I don't believe in Valentine's Day. It's a scam holiday made by greeting card companies to make money off dipsticks like you who believe that giving overpriced paper and chocolate to someone actually means something."

Kevin grabbed Liz's phone and opened it. He showed me a picture of a guy with a Mohawk standing beside a black Mustang.

My eyes bugged.

"Well, he looks like a very nice person."

"Stop it! Kevin!" Liz said, reaching back to try and punch her Sasquatchian sibling.

"He better be nice to you, or Kevin might pay him a visit," I said.

Kevin thumped his chest and growled. I laughed.

Liz cranked a thrashing screamo song by the Quarter Punks on the stereo. The LeRue siblings banged their heads as we drove into a small village of antique and art shops, the kind of place tourists adore in the summer. But on a cold night in February, there wasn't a soul around.

Liz cut the engine and turned off her headlights. The van tires crunched over gravel as we pulled up to an old, leaning house.

Over the front door, in big red letters:

THE DOLL HOSPITAL

"This is a thing people do?" Liz said quietly. "Man, people are weird."

Kevin grumbled in total agreement.

The lights were off. There was a sign in the window: "Dr. Wermling is out."

"I'm going to take a closer look," I said.

The van rocked as Kevin tried to get out with me. I put my hand on his chest.

"Alone, Kevin," I said.

He thumped his chest and pointed at me.

"That's very nice of you. Just keep watch," I said.

Kevin reluctantly sat back in the van with Liz. I
ducked under the building's large picture window
and peered inside. Hundreds of bare doll heads were
haphazardly piled up against the glass. A marionette
dangled from its strings. Old, dusty dolls were on dis-
play in their finest white lace. Cubbyholes were filled
with eyeballs, arms, legs, and stuffed doll torsos.

I climbed a nearby tree to its highest branch so I
could see into the rear window of the doll hospital.

In the middle of the room a doll's body was flayed

open on a small operating room table. Wires from the electrodes attached to the doll ran to a beeping monitor in the corner. Sharp needles stuck out of pincushions on a table full of cutting tools. Metal claws attached to robotic arms splashed into a boiling cauldron and removed a steaming baby doll's head. Water poured from its mouth and eyes.

In the shadows a blond woman raised the doll's head to inspect it.

Then I caught a glimpse of her face in the moonlight. Her skin was stretched and pinched behind her neck, as if she'd had multiple face-lifts. It looked like she was wearing a papery mask under a bright, bleached-blond wig. She was a very ancient person trying to make herself into a human Barbie doll, and the result was just wrong.

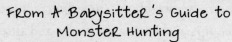

FROM A Babysitter's Guide to Monster Hunting

NAME: Dr. Wermling
OCCUPATION: Doll doctor
LIKES: Dolls, having really puffy duck lips
DISLIKES: Sunshine. The passage of time. Loose stitches.

"Where is that sister of yours?" Dr. Wermling said. "She should have been here with those brats hours ago."

So, this is where Lilly May was going to take the twins. Why here? What's so special about it?

The doctor placed the freshly boiled doll's face on a worktable and twisted it in a vise. She selected a scalpel and scraped her patient's nose, cleaning it with care. She glanced at the clock.

"We'll just have to pay them a visit ourselves," said Wermling.

Dr. Wermling fixed the doll's head to its body and attached electrodes to its head and feet. Then she opened a jar that glowed with an ethereal wisp of purple light. The good doctor carefully plucked the light out with tweezers and inserted it into the doll's open chest. Then she set about threading a needle. Her puffy, fake lips sucked the ends of a red thread. Her trembling hands sewed up the patient's cloth rib cage, trapping the slithering purple glow inside.

Wermling pulled a lever. The electrodes buzzed with bluish light. The doll's back arched. Its limbs sputtered to life. The doctor's eyes flickered purple.

The mad doctor raised her hands. "Rise, Lullu Belle. Rise!"

The doll sat up.

"What a pretty girl you are!" said Dr. Wermling.

Lullu Belle's doll head spun around 180 degrees and stared right at me.

I lost my balance. Clawed the air like a doof and fell out of the tree.

Whoomph! Kevin's thick arms caught me.

"Thanks," I said.

He grunted. *No big deal.*

"Your sister does a lousy job keeping you in check, you know that?"

Kevin and I ran back to Liz in the van. We ducked and watched Wermling drive away from the doll hospital in a station wagon with dolls and teddy bears cluttering the back. Precious Lullu Belle was seated in the front. The doll was wearing a seat belt, glaring out of the passenger window.

"Follow that doll ambulance!" I said.

"On it!" Liz was happy to snap into action, but it turned out to be the world's slowest car chase since the old doctor never drove faster than twenty miles an hour.

"Oh come on!" Liz said. "I can walk faster than this."

We chased (and by "chased" I mean "crept") behind the doctor as she drove past the Renfield house.

I looked at my watch. In one hour my dad was going

to pick me up. We did not have time for this!

Watching from her car, Wermling banged her steering wheel. She checked her watch and slammed on the gas, speeding off at a whopping thirty miles an hour. Liz groaned, and we slowly crawled after her.

The smell of dead fish filled the air as our shadow-ride followed the station wagon into the Innsmouth Marina. Creaking docks stretched into the green fog over the ocean. Liz pulled the van up behind a huge stack of crusty lobster traps.

The docks were empty except for Dr. Wermling and her doll. She stood at the edge of the ocean scratching under her blond wig.

A strange, warm wind picked up, stirring a nearby state flag. In the distance a lonely buoy bell clanked. Kevin whimpered in the back seat. He was peering into the ocean, shuddering.

It was one of the rare times I had ever seen him cower in fear.

"What's wrong, Kev?" Liz asked quietly. Her brother's silvery eyes were fixed on the churning waves. Fog swirled, disturbed by a mountainous shadow approaching the docks.

A masthead shaped like a giant wolf emerged from the wall of mist. I gasped and quickly covered my mouth. A tremendous wooden schooner with full sails glided along the coastline. Shouts and orders were barked on deck. An iron anchor dripping with seaweed plunged into the water. Hulking shadows set about tying the ship to the dock.

"All aboard for Sunshine Island!" came a booming voice.

13

The boat suddenly came alive with red and white lights and bouncy carnival music. A gangplank slid onto the dock. Flags emblazoned with happy suns shot up the mast. Someone was wearing a giant furry frog costume. Beside them, someone else danced on the deck, dressed like a sunshine happy face.

The ghost ship had transformed itself into the world's happiest cruise line. But there was something off about the whole thing. The frog costume didn't fit whoever or whatever was wearing it. The lights bulbs were dim from sea scum. The happy music was out of tune and desperate for joy.

"Is this the ship that took you?" I asked Kevin.

He couldn't even speak. He nodded. *Yes.*

"I'm getting a closer look," Liz said. "Kelly, stay with Kevin."

Low to the ground she zigzagged around the docks. Kevin murmured into his paws, worried for his sister's safety.

"She'll be okay, Kev," I said, patting him on the arm. "She knows what she's doing. But if this is what I think it is, we'll need evidence to show the council."

I grabbed my phone and flicked on the camera. Pinch-zooming onto the ship, I saw the lurking crew bob in and out of shadows. They seemed less human and more like trained baboons.

Beside me, Kevin wiped his giant, sweaty paws through his long brown fur. I wanted to give him a hug and let him know it was going to be okay, but I needed evidence to convince the Council of Babysitters to launch a full-fledged rescue mission. The council was a gathering of very important babysitters who oversaw global babysitting operations. They have the gear, the power, and the resources to do big things. They're sort of like Congress for sitters. If I wanted to undertake a major operation to Sunshine Island, I would need their full support. My trembling fingers tapped the record button, and I aimed it at the horrendous ship.

Clomp. Clomp. Clomp.

The deck shuddered, and the mysterious crew ducked from view before I could see if they were human or monster. The costumed frog and dancing sunshine raised their arms up and held them there, like the best thing ever was about to happen.

A figure strutted onto the deck. A great black tail swayed under a long red coat with gold trim and copper buttons. The claws of a black and gray paw strummed the handle of a sheathed sword.

Baron von Eisenvult, aka the Wolf, stood proudly at the top of the gangplank. He combed back his whiskers and snarled a snout full of sharp, gleaming teeth. Though the walking, talking wolf was terrifying, he was also quite handsome. His eyes held the sparkle of a mastermind. He reminded me of fairy tales where the prince eats the princess and there is no happily ever after.

"Welcome, welcome, welcome," boomed the Wolf.

He was met with silence, and his great big smile turned to a frown. The Wolf stared down at the old woman. His wet snout sniffed the salty air.

"Where are they?" he asked, his voice echoing across the docks.

From where Kevin and I sat, we couldn't hear the quiet woman's response. I pinch-zoomed my camera at the doctor. Her shoulders sagged forward, and she held up the doll as an offering. Von Eisenvult drew his sword and pointed it at the woman's neck.

"You promised me twins," snarled the Wolf.

Kevin yelped and pointed. Liz was shimmying up the rope that tied the ship to the dock.

I gulped as she swung herself onboard.

The Wolf's snout twitched. His eyes narrowed. I could see a smile creeping under his whiskers.

Can he smell us? Does he know we're here? Liz is going to slip and give us away. I didn't shower today, and Kevin definitely didn't. Darn!

"Wait here, Kev," I whispered. "I have to go save your crazy sister."

Kevin yowled as I slipped from the van. I made my way to a row of blue plastic barrels and then stealthily tumbled behind a broken dinghy and tried to get a good shot.

"Liz, you knucklehead!" I whisper-shouted.

I could hear the doll doctor begging. "Please, Baron von Eisenvult, I need more of your wonderful materials," said Wermling, holding up her doll.

The Wolf produced a glowing purple jar. "I held up my end of the bargain. You failed to deliver," snarled the Wolf. "And so I bid you good night. Doctor."

Von Eisenvult's sword slashed. *Snikt! Snikt!* The soap-opera-blond doctor fell to pieces.

Lullu Belle squealed as Wermling collapsed.

I froze. The Wolf had sliced that lady in half.

Stuffing bulged out of the stitches in Wermling's neck and joints. Her torso was made of cloth. Her arms and legs were sewn on with fine red threads. The doll doctor was a doll!

Lullu Belle fell to her fine china knees and patted her maker's arm. Dr. Wermling's eyelids twitched. Her severed hands trailed red thread as they crawled over her body, trying to sew herself back together again. My phone almost slipped from my sweating hands.

"Don't make promises you can't keep," said the Wolf. "And if you wish to stay alive, little doll, next time do as I say and bring me more children. Let's go, crew."

The happy lights died and the jolly flags lowered. The costumed frog and sunshine character took off their foam heads revealing the hideous faces of two goblins. The inhuman crew untethered the ropes. Baron von Eisenvult stalked into the captain's quarters and slammed the door shut behind him.

"Liz!" I hissed. "Get down here!"

Liz clicked her heels together three times and her sneakers lit up. Her rubber soles puckered into suction cups.

"Sitter Sneaks," Liz said. "Boosted them off Mama Vee."

She pressed her feet to the bottom of the masthead,

and they stuck like glue. Hanging upside down, she looked like a punk rock bat.

"Those are really cool, but I'm not getting on that thing without a pair. Put a tracker on the ship and let's go."

"Great idea, genius! Why didn't I think of that? Oh, wait. I did. I don't have one. Do you?"

I patted my jacket even though I knew I didn't have one. I growled in frustration.

A rusty chain clanked as the ship's anchor emerged from the inky water. Portholes thunked open, and rows of yellow eyes sparkled in the dark ship's small windows. Liz looked scared for a second, but then she covered her fear with a scowl.

Oars shot out from the side of the ship and shoved the massive vessel away from the dock. A deep, powerful chant sounded as the rowers strained against the tide.

"Row, row, row your boat, gently down the stream . . ."

Thunka. Thunka. Thunka.

With tiny suctioned steps Liz slowly crawled along the side of the ship to the deck railing. She looked back at me and Kevin. "Hop on, stupid."

Kevin charged to the edge of the dock. He stopped abruptly at the edge of the water, scared to leap into it.

"Merrily, merrily, merrily, merrily, life is but a dream!" chanted the unseen crew.

Liz nervously steadied herself as the ship rocked against the waves. Kevin reached out for his sister.

"Don't go, Kevin. Liz, check your brain cells. The three of us can't ride to some monster island tonight. We need a plan. And gear. We need backup."

"These creeps stole my brother from me, Kelly. It sucked. Now I'm going to burn that stupid island to the ground. With or without you."

Say what you will about Liz LeRue, but she was a fearless warrior.

I waved my cell phone. "I can show this footage to the council, and they'll send an army of babysitters to do it right."

"Those dinosaurs in the head office will never approve it! Trust me, I've tried. Now stop being a follower and start being a leader."

I looked down at the sickly green water. A rowboat was tied to the dock, sloshing in the waves. I loved Kevin and Liz, but they were both a little too insane to pull off this mission on their own. We didn't have the gear. We didn't have a plan. I was not prepared for this level of danger. Judging from Kevin's frazzled, furry expression, neither was he.

Kevin hopped back and forth nervously. Liz shimmied her way to the side of the ship and slipped into an open portal.

"Iiiiz?" he murmured sadly. His giant lower lip trembled.

"Don't do it, Kevin."

Kevin looked from the boat to me and back to the boat. He leaned down, kissed me on the cheek, and then took off running.

"Kevin!"

14

Kevin leaped off the dock and sailed through the air, barely catching the edge of the crusty bow.

Boys. They never listen.

"I'll call you when we dock," Liz said, saluting me as the ship sailed out to sea.

They'll be okay, I said to myself. *Kevin's strong. So is Liz. And she knows what she's doing. And Kevin's been there before. Then again, there's a pretty good chance they both could die moments from now.* As the ship sailed away, I saw its name written on the back in gold: *Serena's Song.*

As in Serena the Spider Queen? As in the bug

lady I squished? I thought. *That is literally not a good sign.*

"You will pay, babysitter!" Lullu Belle's voice rang out.

The little china doll charged at me on her tiny legs. Her porcelain hands were raised in rage.

I picked up a wooden lobster trap and smashed it down over her, trapping Lullu Belle inside the rusty crustacean prison.

I was so not in the mood for another doll fight.

She flailed in the lobster trap's netting as I picked up the trap with the doll inside and tossed it into the back of the babysitter mobile. I scooped up the pieces of the doll doctor and shoved them into the back seat.

"Where's the Wolf going?" I demanded.

"Like I'm telling you," Lullu Belle snapped.

"I melted one of you earlier tonight," I said, shaking the lobster cage. "I'll do the same to you if you don't tell me the truth."

Lullu Belle zipped her lips.

"We can do this the easy way or the hard way."

"Can you fix Dr. Wermling?" Lullu Belle asked sweetly.

"Of course we can," I said, sensing a deal.

I peeled the carpet back from the van floor and placed the lobster cage in a hidden compartment.

"Think about it," I said, shutting the trap door over the doll's face.

I locked it and grabbed Dr. Wermling's severed, crawling hands away from my neck.

"Not so fast." The clawing hands swung from their red threads in my fist.

The nearest container I could grab was an indestructible diaper bag. I stuffed Dr. Wermling's pieces inside. A shudder jolted through my chest. Wermling's glass eyes were staring up at me as I zipped the bag closed.

I checked the time. Only fifteen minutes left to get back to the Renfields!

I called Mama Vee and gave her the twenty-second version of our night, while texting her photographs of the Wolf's nightmare yacht. Aside from all this bad news, it was going to take Mama Vee an hour to get to me, but I had fifteen freaking minutes to get back to the Renfields' house so my dad could pick me up.

Mama Vee put our trusty mechanic and hobgoblin babysitter Wugnot on the phone.

"I've got something that might help," Wugnot said. "It's new tech from the San Fran office. Installed it last week. Look on the dash and you should see a button called remote drive."

A piece of tape on the dashboard marked a red button: Remote Drive.

"Buckle up and press it," Wugnot said.

I pressed the button, and the van's engine rumbled. A camera fixed to the hood blinked on. The gear shift clunked into drive, and the steering wheel spun around with a life of its own.

"Really been wanting to test this thing out. Hang on!" The excitement in Wugnot's voice scared me.

"Test it out?"

I buckled up as the gas pedal was stomped down. The van lunged forward, and I was thrown back in my seat. I was being driven by a lead-footed ghost.

"Car! Car!" I screamed. The van veered onto the road, barely dodging a Dodge.

"I got it," said Wugnot over the van's intercom.

Rocketing down the street, I gripped the door handle and screamed over the phone at Wugnot.

"Just sit back and relax," Wugnot said.

I glanced at the clock. One minute left! So not relaxing!

We made it back to the Renfields' house. I saw my dad's blue Honda of doom pull around the corner.

"Stop!" I shouted.

My driverless van screeched to a stop.

"I cannot wait to get out of this car," I said. "Hey, Wugnot! When you get the van back, there's a nasty doll trapped in a lobster cage and a human-sized one in pieces in the indestructible diaper bag in the back. They might know something so don't play with matches around them."

"What are you implying?" Wugnot asked, playfully defensive.

"Mama Vee told me you like setting toys on fire."

"It's an artistic hobby," Wugnot said.

My dad texted me: **OUTSIDE.**

"Wugnot! We need all the help we can on this. Liz and Kevin could be in huge trouble. I've gotta go!"

I sprang out of the van, somersaulted onto the grass,

and popped up under my dad's window before he could honk the horn.

"Gah! Don't scare me like that!" my dad said, his hands springing into a karate stance.

"You didn't hear me say hi?" I asked innocently, sliding into the passenger seat.

My dad looked around the Renfields' front yard. Luckily, the lights were off. "Dad's getting old, Kelly. Think I'm losing my hearing."

I put a comforting hand on his shoulder and looked back to see the babysitter mobile reversing down the street. The steering wheel reeled the van into a wild U-turn, and it drove off.

"Was that a karate move you did?" I asked.

My dad gave a slow nod. "I've been watching these self-defense tapes. Just in case."

Just in case of monsters.

"I'll protect you, Dad," I said.

He guffawed. "How were the wonder twins?" he asked.

"Double the trouble, double the fun," I said with a shrug. "We played with their Fancy Lady doll."

As we drove back over the bridge, I stared out the window, thinking of Liz and Kevin hiding on a boat full of monsters. How long could they hide until they were found?

103

I typed a superemergency email on my phone, attached every picture and video I had taken of the ship and the Wolf, and sent it to every babysitter I could. Every. Single. One. From Bern to Curtis to the Queen governess herself. Contacting everyone was def going over Mama Vee's head, but this was a big-time emergency. No time for babysitter hierarchy.

I laid out detailed instructions to the nearest chapters prepared for naval assault and asked for them to find *Serena's Song* before it disappeared.

Locate this ship and we will find Sunshine Island.

I hit send and heard the satisfying *whoosh*.

"Did you do anything besides stare at your phone all night?" my dad joked.

I forced a smile.

Now all I have to do is pack my gear; find a boat; make a plan; sneak out; head for Sunshine Island; find Liz, Kevin, and the kids; defeat Professor Gonzalo; not get eaten by the Wolf . . .

The list kept going and going. The one thing I was certain of was that this mission was bigger and badder than anything I had ever done.

15

WHAT IS HER DEAL?

Remove these ugly pics. Please. 🙏

#KellyNoFriends.

DEE-LEETE RED!

Ur so gross I can smell u thru my screen.

W hy on Earth did I check my Facebook page? Or my Instagram? Or my everything else? That morning there were no messages from Liz or Kevin. But my trolls had multiplied. Like monkey poop on a zoo window, their awful comments were smeared everywhere. Even on my Goodreads page. I mean, who trolls someone on Goodreads?

I felt defeated, and it wasn't even eight in the morning.

"Kelly. Breakfast," my dad called.

His voice snapped me out of my scroll trance. I walked down the hall into the kitchen.

"I made blueberry pancakes. I figured since you don't have to rush off to school and I don't have to be at the shop for another hour, we could have breakfast."

I smiled at him. He had a funny way of grounding me.

A melting patty of butter slowly slid down my stack of pancakes.

"What's wrong?" my dad asked.

"My friends are in trouble and people hate me."

"No one hates you," he said. "You're fantastic! You're—seriously now, I'm not just saying this because I'm your dad, but because I see you, and you're doing a pretty good job with the monsters and all. When I was your age the only things I did were play video games and dream about cars."

He leaned closer.

"You know how many times I got in trouble at school?" he whispered. "Let's just say, I was not the best of kids."

My mother whooshed in, dressed in her crisp business best. My father straightened back into his chair.

"Pancakes. Really?" my mom said.

"She's gotta eat, Lex."

My mom pursed her lips. "Empty the dishwasher when it's finished. Take out the trash. Wash your hands. Then start your schoolwork."

"Yes, Mom," I said.

She opened the front door and gasped. Three elderly women wearing tweed cloaks and colorful bonnets stood close together with tight, friendly smiles fixed to their faces.

"Good morning, Mrs. Ferguson," said one leaning on a wooden cane. "I'm sorry to startle you at this hour, darling."

Her accent was super British. It made everything she said sound really important and really smart. They each held up official babysitter badges.

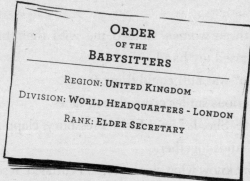

ORDER
OF THE
BABYSITTERS

REGION: UNITED KINGDOM
DIVISION: WORLD HEADQUARTERS - LONDON
RANK: ELDER SECRETARY

"We've come all the way from the London World Headquarters for the Order of the Babysitters." They tucked their IDs back into their shawls.

"I am Elder Pressbury, this is Elder Carbunkle, and that is Elder Doyle."

The ladies nodded in sync.

My eyes widened. I knew those names. They were the three Elder Secretaries to the Queen governess. The top brass. The big cheese.

Elder Pressbury removed her bonnet and bowed her head.

"Might we come in?"

"Careful, Alexa. Remember what happened last time we let some stranger in the house," my dad said. He made a "spider leaping onto his neck" gesture.

"Hi, Mrs. Ferguson," said Mama Vee, stalking up the drive with an apologetic wave.

"I was on my way to work," my mom said, flustered. "We weren't expecting company today. What's this about?"

The three women studied me with their birdlike eyes. I raised my hand.

"Hello" was all I could think to say.

Mysterious smiles crossed their faces.

"There. She. Is," said Elder Pressbury, clapping her gloved hands together.

I didn't know what else to do, so I curtsied. It seemed the royalish and British choice. Turns out I was right because the three Elders curtsied in return.

"We were en route from London when our offices received a high alert from you," Elder Pressbury said, pointing her cane at me.

"We contacted your chapter president, Miss Veronica, who informed us you were grounded, but since these are pressing matters, we told the pilot to bring us here straightaway."

Mama Vee's arms were crossed. She was not pleased.

"Dude, who told you to send out orders to the whole eastern seaboard of babysitters?" Mama Vee whispered. "Everyone was calling me last night, and your phone was off. It's bad enough I have to ask for a crazy amount of funds to rebuild our headquarters, but now you've gone over my head and over Moon's head with this Liz stunt."

"Have you heard from Liz?" I whispered to Vee.

"No. But two babysitters in the Maine chapter who are expert sailors set sail to go searching for the ship because of your email last night. No one's heard from them either."

I gulped.

"Would you like to sit down?" I said, showing them into the living room. "Tea? Or, um, pancakes?"

Elder Pressbury took her time lowering herself onto the couch. A metallic squeak came from her right knee. Only then did I see her leg was a prosthesis.

"I'm sorry but can this wait?" my mom said. "I have to go to work, and Kelly's supposed to be grounded–"

"We need her to speak with the council," said Elder Pressbury. "Today."

"Can she FaceTime?" my mom asked, exasperated.

The women glared back at my mother.

"Two hundred babysitters from around the Western Hemisphere will be gathering at the university in three hours." Pressbury aimed her cane at me again. "Kelly's presence has been requested. So no, she cannot Face-Time."

Nervous bubbles filled my stomach. Speaking before the most powerful babysitters in the world was a huge deal.

"Where is this council meeting?" my dad asked.

"At our North American headquarters. In Manhattan."

My mother threw up her hands. "You have got to be kidding me. Absolutely not."

"Our pilot has assured me she can fly us there in time for the council meeting. But we must leave now to make time. Shall we go?" said Elder Pressbury.

"You people have your own plane?" my father asked, impressed.

"This is a one-time thing," said Mama Vee. "I promise."

"Seems like there are a lot more of those lately," said my mom.

"You and your husband are more than permitted to come to the hearings," pushed Elder Carbunkle. "In fact, we encourage it. If that's okay with you, Kelly?

110

There's even room for you on the plane. But we must go without delay."

"You really have your own plane?" my dad asked.

"We've been fortunate to encounter some very thankful clients," said Doyle, staring at the ground.

"Can we go, Mom? Please?" I asked. I gave my dad powerful puppy eyes.

"It's just a one-hour flight," Mama Vee said.

"I can't," my mother said. "I have work. I can't."

"Kelly will learn much more today outside of this house than she ever could sitting around her room," said Pressbury. "Do you know where the council is meeting?"

"No idea," my mother said. "Sorry, Kelly. But no."

"At Columbia University," said Pressbury.

My mom stopped. Her eyes narrowed.

"You work for the university?" my mom asked.

"We're a secret division dedicated to child care and its various research," said Carbunkle.

"Monster research," Pressbury added. "Invite only."

My mother crinkled her nose. "That's a real college course?"

Mama Vee and the Elders nodded.

"We have offices dedicated to the assistance of monster studies at all the top universities," Elder Pressbury purred. "Oxford. Cambridge. Yale. Princeton. USC."

I swooned.

"Wow," my mom whispered.

"We have been babysitting members of their boards for hundreds of years, and in return they have assisted with many scholarships for our finest sitters. Kelly would be no exception."

My mom crooked her jaw. "The order could get Kelly into a good college?"

"The best," said Pressbury.

"My grades could help, too," I said.

"Indeed. As long as Kelly agrees to keep sitting, she wouldn't have to worry about tuition," said Elder Pressbury.

My mom crossed her arms. She stared at the tiny old ladies.

"Are you bribing me with a full ride to college for my daughter?"

"No student loans. Like, ever?" my dad asked.

The Elders smiled.

"Okay," my mom sighed. "Let's go to New York."

16

We boarded a decommissioned military airplane that looked like the last flight it flew was over Düsseldorf during the Great War. My hair twisted in the propeller wash.

"That's a DC-3!" my dad said over the roar of the sputtering propellers.

The plane looked like it was made out of a tin can.

"I was expecting something a little more James Bond," said my dad.

"Well, my dear, instead you got Jane Bond," said Elder Carbunkle.

"This revolutionized air transport in the nineteen thirties!" said Pressbury, whacking her cane against the airship's warped, metal side where a faded Union Jack was painted.

"They've made a lot of advancements since then!" my dad said.

"We're not made of money, Mr. Ferguson," Elder Carbunkle snapped. "It was a gift from General Hawkins of the RAF for saving his second daughter from the jaws of a Storm Gorgon."

"Is it safe?" my mom asked.

"Very safe!" said Pressbury, ducking into the doorway. "And if anything happens, just grab a parachute. Bad joke. My apologies."

The cabin held seven empty chairs along the metal walls that shook from the deafening engine noise. No Frills Air. No TVs in the seat backs. No flight attendant. No little bags of pretzels.

"Is the governess here?" I asked.

"Her Grace needed to stay in London. Her health has kept her from traveling, bless her soul."

"What's that hissing?" my mom asked.

"Normal!" Elder Pressbury said, covering our ears with radio headsets.

I sat between my father and mother, who was trying to jab her seat belt buckle together.

"Let me," said Mama Vee.

I leaned over and took a selfie of all of us. I sent it to Berna, Curtis, and Cassie.

You're not going to believe where I'm headed!
Wish you guys were coming with! Wish me luck!

"I blame you for this," my mom said to Vee.

Vee didn't say anything. I knew I was going to get a lecture from her later, but for now, Vee had to be cool in front of my parents and the Elders.

My mother kept her eyes fixed on the red light in the ceiling. Her fingers twitched. I knew she was nervously itching for a cigarette even though she had quit years ago.

"Thank you for letting me go to this," I said.

"You're going to think this is normal. That you can just do this kind of thing anytime you want and it's okay. I'm a horrible mother."

"You're the best," I said.

"If they can get you a full ride at a good school, then it's worth it," she said over and over to herself. Good ole Mom. Her fear of me not getting into a good college was stronger than her fear of flying.

The plane shuddered down the runway. Mom grabbed my armrest. My stomach did an antigravity somersault as we lifted into the sky. The plane shook and lurched, but when I looked out the window, we were soaring into the blue sky above a kingdom of clouds.

I opened my notebook and tried to write my speech. The only speech I had ever written was in sixth grade, and it was about why everyone in the world should recycle. I got an A minus. I hoped my plea to launch a mission to Sunshine Island would get the same high marks.

All you have to do is speak from the heart, and everyone will understand. Liz and Kevin will finally be safe. The kids and mutants will be freed. And we'll all live happily ever after.

A line of babysitters, wearing sunglasses and black suits, waited by a convoy of station wagons at the small airport outside of the city. As we followed signs toward Manhattan, I couldn't sit still. I was supposed to be in social studies right now, and here I was, heading into the Big Apple! A place I had only known from myth and legend, and by that I mean TV and rom-coms.

In the front seat, Mama Vee proofread my speech and gave it back to me.

"Is it good?"

"It's not a question if it's good. Of course it's good. You're smart and a great leader," said Vee. "It's a question if they'll allow it."

The convoy of station wagons drove us into a canyon of skyscrapers, and there, we beheld Columbia University. It felt like summer camp for almost grownups. The campus was gorgeous. The marble columns, the giant steps. Students were smiling and drinking steaming coffee with each other in their pajamas. It was the total opposite of the real world we had driven through.

"This way, darlings," said Pressbury, marching toward a three-story Gothic building covered in a wall of ivy. While the other sitters made sure no one was watching, a sitter in sunglasses removed an antique key that had been retrofitted with a microchip in the center.

Sunglasses slid the key into the mouth of an ogre statue hidden in the leafy greenery. She pulled back on the wall, and a secret door opened up.

I clenched my speech in my sweaty hand as we entered the North American headquarters of the Order of the Babysitters.

The Elder Secretaries led us up a winding staircase that passed corridors where I caught glimpses of monster bone displays and a large aquarium where a mermaid swam in circles. I wanted to stop and gawk, but the Elders rushed us into a huge lecture hall that was guarded by two babysitters (yes, wearing sunglasses) with little earpieces in their ears. Inside were circular rows of seats filled with babysitters from around the world. There must have been two hundred women and men, and a few good monsters. I froze as all two hundred rose to their feet. All eyes were on me.

Elder Pressbury took my hand and led me toward the stage. The others escorted my parents to their seats. I looked over my shoulder and saw my mother and father give me a good luck wave. An antique-looking wooden podium sat in the middle of the small circular stage in the center of the great chamber, and it felt like I was walking onto a gigantic eyeball.

Mama Vee and I sat among other top brass babysitters wearing their finest outfits. I was clearly not dressed for the occasion. My Converse shoelaces were untied. My nubby green sweater had a mustard stain on the sleeve, and my jeans were about a week late for laundry day. I pulled my hair back into a poufy ponytail and sat up straight trying to look dignified and respectable.

The council members looked like they were in their fifties or older. Where were all the cool students we'd seen outside? Why weren't they here?

Man, I wish Berna and the gang were here. I wanted to FaceTime the whole thing, but I had a feeling that would be kind of a party foul.

A sitter in sunglasses shut the giant wooden doors with a boom. Elder Pressbury creakily walked to the podium.

"Thank you all for coming from far and near. I hereby call to session the Order of the Babysitters Council."

She slammed her cane onto the ground.

"At this time, the council would like to invite our sister sitters from Florida to speak about the mysterious appearance of an abominable snowman on their beaches."

A babysitter from Los Angeles got up and spoke about a toxic Scumsucker that had appeared in the L.A. River. Then we heard from a babysitter from Indiana, where an outbreak of Oozers was threatening to swallow up kids in the cornfields. At the end of each discussion, the problem was resolved and action was promised. This went on for hours.

I was beginning to think they had forgotten about me.

I mean, Liz and Kevin needed our help immediately. But it seemed like everyone around the world had monster problems.

"And now we'll hear from Kelly Ferguson and Veronica Preston of the Rhode Island chapter."

I cleared my throat and stood up beside Mama Vee.

"You want to go first?" I asked.

"It can wait. You go, kiddo," said Mama Vee.

I had an out-of-body experience as I walked up to the podium. All these faces were staring at me. This was my moment. My big chance to safeguard the future of kids around the world.

I sat my notebook on the old podium and adjusted the microphone.

Don't screw this up. Stop saying negative things. You can do this.

"Esteemed members of the Order of the Babysitters, um, Council," I began.

Coughs in the crowd were followed by snot-filled hacking.

"My friends, er, colleagues and I have made a recent discovery about an island of monsters located off the coast of Maine called Sunshine Island. This is a horrible place and poses a great threat to the children who have been taken there. Up until now, the island's location remained a mystery. But thanks to the brave actions of Rhode Island chapter vice president, Liz LeRue, and her brother, Kevin LeRue, we will soon know Sunshine Island's exact location. My proposal is this: we send a team of highly trained babysitters to the island on a fact-finding mission, gather information, retrieve Liz and Kevin LeRue and the other missing kids, and then return to the council for further investigation while we reunite the stolen children with their families."

"Oh, is that all?" Elder Doyle whispered.

"But we must act now and we must act swiftly," I said. "The lives of good babysitters and good kids are at stake. Thank you."

Elder Pressbury grabbed my shoulder and held me in place as she leaned into the microphone.

"You have heard her request," said Pressbury. "What sayeth the council?"

Two hundred bells rang at once.

Everyone had an opinion.

"That would cause a war," said a fifty-year-old babysitter.

"We've never invaded monster territory," called out a babysitter wearing a headscarf.

"Babysitters are warriors of peace. We do not start wars," another babysitter pointed out.

I felt like I was standing in front of a verbal firing squad. I saw my mom and dad exchange upset looks.

"I don't want to start a war," I said. "I want to help out a few kids. Liz and Kevin could be in trouble."

"You're a child," Elder Pressbury said. "Leave these things to the adults."

"She knows nothing of the Wolf that haunts that island!" bellowed Elder Carbunkle.

"You mean Baron von Eisenvult?" I said into the mic. "Yeah. I saw him."

"You saw Baron von Eisenvult?" asked a nervous babysitter.

"Last night," I said.

Everyone gasped.

"I sent you guys an email about it," I said.

"I haven't checked my email since yesterday," shot back the nervous one.

"We're not addicted to our phones like the youths of today."

I groaned.

"Baron von Eisenvult is back!" I said.

The council gasped. Elder Pressbury touched her right knee, where her prosthesis began. "After our last encounter with the Baron, many, many lives were lost. On both sides. Von Eisenvult lost his first wife and his cubs. He surrendered, and we babysitters signed an agreement stipulating that in exchange for him staying on his island and living in exile, we would leave him in peace. The Baron has since lived on that island, eating herds of sheep and keeping to himself."

"What about the kids there?"

She sadly shook her head. "Mutants. Monsters. We have no cure for them."

Wow. How could they be so coldhearted?

"And you're okay, letting him eat his herds of sheep in exile?"

"As long as he does not show his snout again, yes."

"Well, it looks to me like he's out of retirement," I snapped. "And I'm not going to let my friends be his herds of sheep. Look, I know what I'm asking for isn't easy, but we can do it together. This is a bit of a humble brag, but my friends and I did defeat the Grand Guignol on Halloween. And the rest of us took down the Spider Queen on Christmas."

"So, what's your strategy for this mission?" asked Pressbury.

I held up my file folder full of Kevin's drawings and our pieced-together map of Sunshine Island. "I have it here, and I sent it in the email."

"Did you send it to my AOL account?" called out a grumpy babysitter.

"How can we vote if we haven't read the file?"

"We should adjourn to read the file," croaked a voice from the stands.

"Send the recon pixies!"

"Yes! Send the recon pixies!"

"Need I remind the council we sent the entire Sparkle Brigade ten years ago? None of those recon pixies came back alive," warned Pressbury.

"Don't forget the horrors of the War of the Five Tentacles!"

"We have finally found balance with the Baron. There is peace."

I banged my fist on the oak podium. "And I'm telling you, peace is about to get a whole lot worse. The Baron is up to something. The Big Bad Wolf has evil plans in motion."

"What proof have you of this evil plan?"

"A doll told me."

A chorus of snorts and chuckles. "Evil dolls are not to be trusted. Check the guide."

"Check the guide!"

My heart was in the back of my throat. Gulping didn't help get rid of it.

"How dare you?" said Mama Vee, standing at my side. "This young lady had the courage and conviction to come here and ask for your help and this is how you act? I'm shocked and disappointed at what this council has become."

There was quiet. No coughing. No yelling.

They're listening.

"If Kelly says there's a storm coming, then you better get your umbrellas because this kid is the finest, most exceptional babysitter I have ever known. So stop talking and listen."

Mama Vee looked at me and winked.

"All yours, kiddo," she said.

I took a deep breath. I held that breath. It lifted me up.

Speak your heart, Kelly.

"I love kids, and I want to help things grow, and I know, I know—it sounds supercheesy and everyone says this—but I really want to make the world a better place," I said. "The head of the Boogeypeople is bringing more kids to Sunshine Island for a reason. The Wolf is on the prowl again. I know it seems like Kevin LeRue and the other mutants on that island are a lost cause, and maybe they are the bad kids, but they're still kids. And they need our help," I insisted. "The parents of those kids deserve to see their children again."

"All those in favor of landing on Sunshine Island and causing the next great monster war, say aye," Pressbury said calmly.

A few sitters rang their bells and voted for me, including Mama Vee. I gave them each a thankful nod. But the vast majority of the council held silent.

"Opposed?" sang Pressbury.

A resounding "nay" shook the lecture hall.

"The council has spoken. Rejected."

She stomped her cane on the ground.

The council stomped their feet along with her. I looked at Mama Vee. She hung her head.

"Why did you bring me here?" I asked, glaring at Pressbury. "Was it to humiliate me?"

She reached out a bony finger and pressed it to my heart. "You want to make the world a better place? So do we."

Elder Pressbury reached down. *Snap. Twist. Thunk.*

She placed her prosthetic limb onto the podium. We all stared at it for, like, a whole minute.

"But you see, my dear," Pressbury said, nodding at her rubber leg, "that is what happens when you go up against the Big Bad Wolf."

18

After a loud but uneventful flight home in the flying Pepsi can, Mama Vee dropped me and my parents off at our house.

"I'll notify you as soon as I hear anything from Liz or the Maine chapter," she said. "Good night, Fergusons. You guys rock."

"You spoke well, honey," my mom said. "I was proud of you."

"Life just gets more and more bizarre," my dad said with a yawn.

"Straight to bed," my mom said. "Tomorrow you're doing double-duty chores to make up for what you didn't do today."

I gave her a long hug and walked to my room.

I listened for the sound of my father's snore before I crept down the hall to the desk where the family computer awaited.

Don't check Facebook. Don't check Facebook.

I checked Facebook.

FAILURE 4 LIFE!

Spineless AND hideous.

DELETE UR LIFE.

I growled and was about to log off when . . .

Ding!

A message from Liz! My heart jumped.

A series of pictures.

The first picture was murky and blurry. I could make out a glowing sign: "BELL LABS."

Berna was right! Bell Labs was on the way to Sunshine Island!

I clicked on Liz's second picture. There were colorful lights twinkling on the horizon.

Looks like they're approaching the island.

The third picture was of hideous goblin faces scowling into the camera.

They got caught!

Like a tiny candle flickering inside of me. They were still alive. But they definitely needed a hand.

I Google Mapped Sunshine Island.

It was so small. How could it possibly be home to some of the world's most deadly monsters?

I unfolded the map Kevin drew of the island and held it up to the screen. They were a squiggly match.

I plugged my headphones into the family computer and Skyped Berna. She connected me to Cassie, Curtis, and Victor.

"We need to mobilize," I said.

"I can't let you go alone," said Berna. "You're my date to the dance."

"¿Qué?" Victor asked.

"I'm going to the dance with Berna, Victor," I said.

"Unless you have anything you'd like to say?" Berna asked.

Victor shook his head.

"Did you call us to talk about the dance or to talk about starting Wolf War Three?" Curtis said.

"We need to act and we need to act now," I said. "Before it's too late."

"It'sh againsht the rulesh, and you don't have a boat or a shmall army of babyshittersh," Cassie said.

"We *are* a small army of babysitters," said Curtis. His chipped front tooth poked out of his big, goofy smile.

"Thanks, Curtis," I said. "But I don't want to put anyone's life at risk."

"Liz and Kevin are my friends too," said Curtis.

"My parentsh will never let me go," said Cassie.

"Mine either," said Victor. "But that doesn't mean we shouldn't go. We're the only ones who can do something and so we should. If that means my family is mad at me, let them be mad. I have seen many children taken from their families and I could not do anything. Now I can."

"Dude knows how to make a speech," Curtis said.

"Shay you do run away from home, break the Tenth Law, and decide to go to thish island. How are you going to get there, geniush?" Cassie asked.

I chewed my headphone cord.

"I've been thinking about this. From here to the island, it's a four-hour boat ride. No ferries go there, obviously. I was thinking we could charter a boat. I've been saving up money for summer camp. But maybe I could use it to like hire some kind of ship to take us to the island?"

"We could say we're studying to be fishermen," Curtis said. "My cousin got his GED in fishery. When he gets out of prison, he's gonna catch big tuna."

"No way," Berna said. "I don't want to put some poor, innocent boat rental person in danger."

"Right," I said, picking a piece of headphone cord off my tongue. "We'll find a boat."

"Are you guysh hearing yourshelvesh?" Cassie spat.

"The council voted no. That'sh it. If you break the rulesh, you'll be kicked out of the order."

"We'll go and get Liz and Kevin back and see what kind of operation we're dealing with," I said.

"If we go to Sunshine Island, we need to be prepared," said Berna.

Curtis snapped his fingers in excitement. "My dad built this zombie apocalypse bunker in the backyard. Just in case. I've got tons of camping equipment. We have all the gear. Tents. Canteens. Sleeping bags."

"Great! It'll be just like a camping trip. But with defensive tactical gear and assorted monster hunting equipment," I said. "And I'll bring the snacks. I'm great at snacks."

"I'm bringing my crossbow," Curtis said.

"We still need a way to the island," Berna said.

Victor cleared his throat. He chewed his thumbnail. "My uncle has a fishing boat."

My heart lifted. "You do? He does?"

"One time, we were caught in a terrible hurricane," Victor added. "I helped my family pilot back to shore."

I cocked my head. "Really? You never told me that."

"You never asked," he said.

"High five for my man, Victor!" Curtis shouted. "Hook it up!"

Berna clacked away. "Local weather report says calm seas and low winds are expected tomorrow morning."

"Guysh. Are we really going to do this? Please shay no," said Cassie.

"If we don't, who will?" I asked.

Dear Mom and Dad

Good morning!

Or good afternoon or good evening, depending on when you figure out that I set up a dummy in my room to make you think I was still at home. Surprise! I thought it was a pretty good dummy, given my limited resources.

Anyhoo. If you've found this letter, let me start off by saying I'm sorry for faking you out with the dummy and sneaking out of the house without telling you. I had to go on a short but important "field trip." I will be careful and do my best to stay out of harm's way. If all goes well, we should be home sometime tomorrow. I'm hoping it will be sooner, but I don't want to get your expectations up. Try not to worry. In fact, I hope you have no idea I'm even gone because I know just how much trouble I will be in when I get back.

And, Mom, even though you might be supermad right now, please don't start smoking. Try not to worry. Babysitters are trained for this kind of thing.

Your loving daughter,

Kelly

19

Victor's uncle's boat whooshed over the glassy water. The sun was strong. It felt good and warm with the cold ocean wind. My hair was doing a wild dance until Victor threw me a green baseball hat from inside the cabin. I handed everyone a juice box and a snack, then I sat back with Berna. We pulled on our sunglasses, checked the map, and watched the shoreline drift by while we munched potato chips.

Cassie stood on the bow of the ship and tried to get Curtis to impersonate that scene from *Titanic* with her, but Curtis was not having it. Victor smiled at me from the captain's wheel.

For a moment we were kids playing hooky to go fishing. I blasted a reggae song from my phone and took a few selfies with the gang.

"I can't believe you, uh, *borrowed* your uncle's boat," I said to Victor.

"My parents are right. You are a bad influence," he joked.

"We should have told Mama Vee," Berna said quietly to me.

"I left her a note, too," I said.

"I mean, she should be here. With us," Berna said.

I shook my head. "By the time we convinced Vee to come, Liz would have been turned into a monster," I insisted.

Berna narrowed her eyes. I could tell she disagreed with me but it was too late. We were on our way.

"Can we, gurp, shlow d-d-down, pleashe?" Cassie said.

Her face had turned yellowish green. She swallowed like she had a funny taste in her mouth.

"Keep your eyes on the horizon," Victor called back. "Sometimes helps."

Cassie's glassy eyes locked on to the distant horizon. She was fighting something lurching up inside of her. Curtis tried to help Cassie, but she shoved him away and hurled. Berna and I held Cassie's head and wiped her mouth. I gave her a sleeve of saltines and a can of Coke.

"That'sh better," she said.

Berna handed out copies of Kevin's map that she had superimposed over the Google map of Sunshine Island.

"Pop quiz, babysitters," Berna said. "Which side of the island are we entering on?"

I pointed to the right side of the map, at the mine and prison camp. "From the intel Kevin gave us about Sunshine Island, we know kids are kept in a prison right by this mine. Liz and Kevin would most likely be kept there."

Berna tapped the corner of the island. "Our best point of entry is here. We keep away from the amusement park and the wild woods, and we get right into the prison. We can get Liz and Kevin and who knows how many out."

Three hours later, we were sailing into deeper sea. A haze covered the sky. The waves picked up, but Victor expertly sliced the boat through them. The sun slid behind ragged clouds.

The temperature dropped. I zipped up my jacket and saw a patch of land with a looming redbrick industrial fortress squatting on it.

"Bell Labs, you guys!" I said, pointing at the letters on the side of the building. We checked the map and high-fived. We were on the right path.

Victor checked his GPS. "Sunshine Island is twenty minutes away."

"Better gear up," I said.

Berna unzipped the saddlebags she brought. Because sitter headquarters was temporarily staying at her house, Berna had access to all the sitter tech the order had sent over to keep us in stock.

Curtis smeared his face with camouflage makeup and checked his crossbow. Berna spit out her old gum and popped in a fresh piece of Blueberry Burst. She

The Sitter Swords

Night-vision binoculars

The Creature Crossbow

Mama's Mean Machetes

The K.O. Club

The Detonating Ducks

The Slimeball Slugger

pulled a red scarf over her forehead.

A cold, damp air fell over the boat.

"Sunshine Island," Victor said. "Dead ahead."

"Pleashe don't shay 'dead,'" Cassie mumbled.

I peered into the mist, but I couldn't see any sign of the island. The GPS and the map insisted it was here. Victor steered to the east as we stood on the deck, tensely fixing our eyes into the fog.

I peered through Berna's binoculars and saw the

peak of a rusty roller coaster rising through the cloud cover.

Beep. Beep.

The boat's radar.

On the small black screen, digital orange blotches looked like they were coming toward us.

Beep. Beep.

"Something's out there," Victor whispered.

We gripped our weapons. The boat sloshed back and forth in the dark gray water.

The orange blips on the radar trailed closer to the center of the screen. Whatever was coming was ten times the size of our little boat.

Beep. Beep.

"It's here," Victor said. "Right under us."

"Go fashter!" Cassie said.

"I'm trying to steer away from it. It could be coral," Victor said. "I don't want to crash my uncle's boat."

"Or it could be a three-ton sea slug thinking we're its next meal," Berna said, looking over the edge.

"Or a pack of cannibal mermaids," Curtis said with strange glee, leaning over the railing.

I peered into the murky water. Something was down there. Something yellow.

"You guys!" I pointed at the ocean.

A plastic mustard bottle tangled in a web of trash

bags bubbled to the surface.

I exhaled with relief. Discarded water bottles clunked against the hull of the boat. Empty potato chip bags and burger wrappers undulated across the waves. At first it looked like someone had dumped their garbage overboard, but the junk kept growing. All around us, the ocean was filled with trash.

Victor stopped the engine. "If this gets caught in the propeller, it's game over."

He passed around oars.

"We have to paddle through it," Victor said.

We sludged quietly through old sneakers and waves of plastic straws.

"This is crazy," I said.

"I did my science report on the Great Pacific garbage patch," Berna said. "They're, like, everywhere now."

A hillside of cardboard Amazon delivery boxes loomed like an iceberg. A warped blanket of melted Fiji water bottles shimmered in pools of rainbows. The fog we had been seeing was a toxic mist hissing off the mishmash of chemicals in the trash.

My eyes watered. Berna coughed. Cassie wheezed. The boys gagged.

"Look!" said Victor.

Twenty feet away, bobbing half-sunken in the

garbage, was a sailboat. I recognized the name: *No Worries*.

"That's the Maine sitters' boat!" I said. "Hello!"

The sailboat was tilted, trapped in the muck. A hole had been ripped out of its hull.

"Where do you think they went?" Cassie asked.

My oar jerked to a stop, caught in a sinewy tangle of plastic wires and black seaweed. I yanked it. Something yanked back.

The wiry sludge coiled around the oar and stretched like elastic.

The boat lurched. Something below knocked into us. We swayed in the sludge.

The radar screen was completely orange.

"It'sh under the trash!" cried Cassie.

"No," I said. "It *is* the trash."

FROM A Babysitter's Guide to Monster Hunting

NAME: The gyre, trash vortex

TYPE: Spontaneous sentient evil

WEIGHT: 50 tons

LENGTH: A mile

ORIGIN: Made up of stuff people buy, mixed with seawater—is a dangerous, toxic combination

LIKES: Swimming, eating more trash, growing more trash. Landfills. The world's obsession with bottled water and plastic packaging. Flies. Litterbugs.

DISLIKES: Neat freaks, recyclers

WEAKNESSES: "Do Not Litter" signs

FUN FACT: A horror movie was made about the very first gyre back in the 80s. The film was a huge flop because no one believed they could be real. The movie was also a musical. It has since become a cult classic.

WARNING: When the garbage patch belches three times in a row, seek solid ground.

The boat surged out of the water. We slid forward, clinging to each other, and suddenly, we were lifted ten feet high. We screamed as the sea blob tipped the boat into its mushy grip.

The bow smashed into a pool of Styrofoam containers and plastic sporks. Fingers made from thousands of plastic straws grabbed at us.

"Frag out!" Curtis cried.

He twisted the head of a rubber ducky and launched it into the ocean of garbage.

A geyser exploded, sending muck-monster chunks flying.

An otherworldly squeal rippled through the garbage patch. Stretchy trash tentacles lashed out at us. We hacked through its gooey limbs.

I hurled a rubber ducky depth charge in front of the boat. *Boom! Squeal!* A small path cleared in front of us. Curtis lobbed another ducky that tore a huge hole in the gyre.

Victor gunned the engine. Behind us, a mountain of trash surged into a fifteen-foot wave. Victor veered the boat as the dripping sludge smashed into the water. The island came into view. The rocky shore was close. We could make it.

The boat jerked to a stop. The engine made an angry, straining grind. A web of garbage wrapped around the boat propeller. Cassie raised her machete to try to cut us loose.

Three distinct burps broke the blob's surface. We were dragged sideways.

Waves of plastic shopping bags swirled into a circle. The ocean was a merry-go-round of junk, spinning us in dizzying circles.

"Trash vortex!" I screamed.

A hole widened in the center of the garbage patch as it sucked junk down its gullet like a hungry bathtub drain. The gyre was reeling us in. We were the catch of the day.

I looked around for any sign of hope.

"We need to jump," I said.

"Go in the water?!" Berna shouted. "Are you crazy?"

"Shore's right there. We can make it if we swim real fast. But if we stay on this boat, we're going straight down the garbage disposal."

"Well, I can't swim that fast," Berna said.

"I can!" said Curtis.

He pulled off his shirt and his jeans, and so help me, he was wearing a scuba diving suit underneath his clothes.

"Have you been wearing that all day?" Cassie asked.

Curtis pulled on his babysitter backpack and pressed a button on the shoulder strap. Two fins shot out of the side of his book bag, and a compact dive scooter sprang out of the back.

"The Seaside Sitter Dive Scooter," Curtis said. "I've been waiting a long time to use this."

The dive scooter's propeller whistled.

Curtis strapped a scuba mask over his face. "All ashore that's going ashore!"

Everyone stared in shock as he dove into the water.

"That boy is crazy," sighed Berna.

Cassie yelped. "Don't you leave me, Curtish Critter!"

Berna grabbed Cassie's hand and waited until the boat circled around so it faced shore. "Kelly, you take loverboy. Cass, you're coming with me."

"I hate all of you! We're going to die!"

"Shut up, Cassie!"

"I can't leave my uncle's boat!" Victor said, clinging to the wheel.

"We'll come back for it!" I said, and took his hand.

We ran to the end of the boat. The gyre's growing gullet gurgled behind us like a black hole.

Victor squeezed my hand, and together we jumped. My body shot with tingles. The waves were ice cold. I kicked my feet. Strange tendrils touched my sneakers. Water thrashed. Something snatched my backpack, and I was dragged under the ocean, flailing and screaming.

"Swim!"

Berna had grabbed my backpack. Everyone held on to Curtis, and his Seaside Sitter Dive Scooter pulled us away from the vortex, kicking and thrashing.

Victor looked back to see the trash vortex swallowing his uncle's boat whole. That seemed to satisfy the gyre's hunger. Its ripples and bulges settled with a long, steamy sigh.

We dragged ourselves onto the rocky beach and caught our breaths.

"My uncle's boat!" Victor said, staring out into the water.

"Forget your boat," Berna said. "How are we going to get home?"

The woods along the shore were tall and thick. Strange whistles and insect noises chirped within its darkness.

"We'll have to find another vehicle and commandeer that home," I said, wringing water out of my hair.

"Oh, is that all we have to do?" Victor snapped.

"Victor, I'm sorry. If your uncle's insurance doesn't cover his boat being swallowed by a monster, then, well, I've been saving up to go to Camp Miskatonic. You can use my camp funds to pay for the boat."

Victor shook his head angrily. This was not going well.

"Supply check," Berna said.

Luckily, our babysitter packs were waterproof, so most of our gear was protected.

I looked around for my cooler full of food.

"Lost the snacks," I said sadly.

"The shnacksh are gone?" Cassie cried. "I wash really looking forward to having shome Pringlesh. That'sh it. I'm shending a distresh call."

She removed her clunky sitter satellite phone.

"A distress call for snacks?" Curtis said. "I don't think they'll deliver."

"You're hilarioush," Cassie said, and dialed. "Mama Vee and the order will have to come get ush."

"Wait, wait," I said. "We only just got here. We can't give up. We have to carry on with the mission."

"You sound like Liz," Curtis said.

He meant it as a compliment, but it came out as an insult. Liz was always the crazy one.

Am I the new crazy one? I thought I was Kelly Ferguson, reasonable Mathlete who liked watching Korean dramas. Maybe I was not as nice and calm as I thought I was.

"Your confidence, while reckless, is inspiring, Kelly," Berna said, "but I'm with Cassie. We're stranded on a monster island. We're going to have to suck it up and call for help."

I exhaled heavily and looked at the map. We had failed before we even began.

But they were right. Best to make preparations and sacrifice my pride.

"Make the call," I said.

Cassie dialed her sitter sat-phone and pointed it at the sky.

"No shignal. We need to get away from theesh treesh and get to higher ground to shend out a call," said Cassie.

"And then try to find Liz and Kevin," I said.

Everyone shivered in their squishy sneakers.

"We can do this, guys," I said. "We stay together

and we stay cool and we stay strong. We can do this."

Everyone grumbled half-heartedly.

"Captain's right. We got the skills to pay the bills," Curtis said, and unsheathed the biggest hunting knife any of us had ever seen. "Fourteen inches of stainless-steel power. Can cut through metal, glass, and bone."

"Good news, guys! My bottle rocket made it!" Victor said, holding up a puny little bottle rocket and a book of matches he had sealed in a sandwich bag.

"It's a rescue mission, not the Fourth of July, bro," Curtis said.

"Looks like the compound is this way," said Berna. "No. Wait." She turned the map around several times. "Sorry. My GPS is on the fritz. Something on the island's messing with it. I'm getting a real Bermuda Triangle vibe from this place. That way!"

A graveyard of wrecked boats from all different eras, from schooners to tugboats, had washed up along the shore. We checked them for radios, but their insides had been gutted.

Into the woods. Hazy shafts of sunlight beamed through the thick, thorny treetops.

Keeping a tight diamond formation like we learned in training, with our hands on our weapons and our eyes on alert, we crossed creeks running with bubbling, smelly tar. The atmosphere should have been freezing, but somehow a tropical heat radiated through the island.

Cassie waved her sitter sat-phone around but still couldn't pick up a signal.

"Keep your eyes peeled," I whispered. "Who knows what kind of defenses this island has."

Three huge stones carved into the shape of claws jutted out from the earth. It looked like a giant foot was buried in the ground. We passed a misty waterfall where a huge carving of a monster hand reached out from behind the water.

Farther up we found a private jet that had nose-dived into the ground. Claw marks were torn across its wings. While Curtis checked the plane for a radio, I saw that it had crashed beside an enormous stone face overgrown with roots and vines. It depicted a hideous, thorny-crowned creature with twenty-foot-wide eye-balls peering up at us.

"This thing must have been huge when it was standing," I said, looking back at all the scattered pieces of the statue.

A shadow streaked behind us. Leathery wings flapped. We looked skyward.

Through the canopy of twisted branches and thorns, massive bat-like wings rode the wind. Talons skimmed the treetops.

Dread seized my heart. I held up my fist, and everyone froze.

Gargoyles. Do not let that thing see you. It could rip us all to shreds.

Its glowing red eyes scanned the horizon and then looked downward.

I pointed to the eye of the monster statue.

We need to hide right now.

Keeping their eyes on the sky, Berna, Cassie, Victor, and Curtis followed after me as I ducked inside the statue's hollow, cavernous head. We huddled together in the shadows. Higher up in the sky, a second gargoyle banked through the air, making wide turns with the icy calm of a vulture.

Berna snapped a picture of it and quickly pressed herself against the stone wall.

A third monster wove figure eights around its pals. In the quiet I heard Berna's grip tighten on her weapon. Victor's breathing was fast and trembling. The three gargoyles patrolled the skies. Their wings raced like rippling kites.

I quietly flipped open the *Babysitter's Guide to Monster Hunting.*

NAME: Gargoyle

TYPE: Elemental Class 2

STRENGTHS: Swooping; slicing; stealth; frightening people; staying still for a long, long time; guarding a castle. Very, very patient. Do not get in a staring contest with them. Hearing.

WEAKNESS: Being turned into stone. Long-distance travel. Fire. HOT FIRE.

For five minutes no one spoke. The gargoyles soared higher and higher until the whoosh and flap of their wings faded away.

"Wingspan on those things must be twelve feet," Curtis whispered.

"Fifteen," whispered Cassie.

"Think they know we're here?" Victor asked.

"If they knew we were here, we'd be dead," I said.

We climbed out of the statue's head and darted into the woods. The ground grew steeper as we trudged uphill. Five creatures waited among the trees. I gasped and held up my fist.

Peering through Berna's binoculars, I saw five bizarre, crumbling monster statues tilting in the dirt like uneven tombstones.

The creepy carvings stood at the entrance of a fallen temple overgrown with ivy. Crows dotted the sagging rooftop. The building was enormous.

Darkness beckoned inside its crumbling columns. No one dared move another muscle.

"Dude. Queen B. Where is the compound?" I asked.

Berna checked the map and chewed her gum slowly.

"Are we losht?" Cassie said.

"No!" Her voice raised an octave.

"You're not inshpiring confidensh, Berna," Cassie said.

"We should keep our voices down," said Victor,

watching the temple crows.

"It's not my fault!" Berna said. "That trash monster threw us off course."

"But you're the great navigator!" Cassie spat.

"Quiet!" I shouted. "If we're going to get through this, we need to be a team. It's not Berna's fault we're lost."

"We're not lost," Berna mumbled. "We're somewhere."

"Where?" I snapped.

Berna pointed to the left side of the island on the map.

"That's the exact opposite side of the island we need to be on, Bern," I said.

"I realize this," Berna said through her clenched teeth.

She held up her compass. It spun in circles. "The island is messing with my compass. North is south, and south is north. I should have figured that out, but it took me a moment to get my bearings. I'm good now, though. I got this."

Curtis grabbed the map from her. "I think she's right. Then again, I'm the one following you guys."

"Great," I said. "Now we have to cross the amusement park to get to the compound."

"You said we were going for higher ground," Berna said.

"We are, but I also want to get to Liz and Kevin and the kids."

"Kelly, we're in serious trouble here, and you're act-
ing like we're at summer camp," Berna said.

"I'm just trying to help our friends," I said.

"What about the friends right in front of you?" she
asked.

"You mean the friends who got us lost?" I snarked.

Berna glared at me. "Oh, I'm sorry if I'm reading a
map, drawn by a fourteen-year-old monster, I might
add, wrong while on an island designed to drive me
crazy! You think you can do a better job?"

I locked eyes with her. We were having our first best
friend fight, and I did not like it. Not only were we
scared, I could feel the island's weird energy messing
with us.

"You're doing fine," I said, eager to cut the tension
between us. "Let's keep moving."

We walked around the temple, keeping clear of its
vaulted columns. I caught a glimpse of a towering wall
inside. Ancient hieroglyphs were chiseled into the marble. I was drawn toward the wall, pulled by its dark,
magnetic presence.

"Kelly, don't go in there," Victor said.

My hand reached out as I glided into the temple.
The carvings showed monsters bowing at the foot
of an enormous, impossibly giant monster that was
emerging from the earth.

As my fingers brushed an etching, a low chant

rumbled in the dark corridors of the temple.

Victor grabbed my shoulder and swung me around. The chanting stopped suddenly.

"What's wrong with you?" he said.

I blinked. "What do you mean?"

"We've been calling your name for three minutes! I didn't know where you went," he said, escorting me into the sunlight, away from the monstrous wall.

"Weird," I said, joining the others. "I didn't hear you guys."

"You okay? We can't have you spacing out on us now, Ferguson," Berna said.

"We were yelling for you," Cassie said with her hands on her hips.

Berna studied me with serious concern. I was going to tell them about the gigundo monster on the wall and how it looked like the enormous statue we had passed, when there was an explosion of dead leaves.

A wild-faced woman had shot out from the dirt. Her clothes were ragged. Her eyes were crazed. I raised my sword.

"Babysitters? It's me!" she shrieked. "Emmy Banks!"

We held our weapons high.

"Who?" Curtis said.

"Emmy! Chapter president of the Order of the Maine Babysitters." Her voice was hoarse and raspy, as if she had been screaming all day and night. "We got an emergency request from a sitter named Kelly Ferguson."

"That's me!" I threw my arms around the lost, crazy-looking babysitter. I introduced Emmy to everyone. I gave her my canteen, and she guzzled it, water spilling down her chin.

"Thanks for coming," I said.

"My vice president, Jenny, and I took out our boat, not thinking we'd ever see what we saw. This incredible ship sailing into the moonlight . . . with a wolf at the wheel. We followed it all the way here, but then . . . we weren't expecting the trash monster."

"Neither were we," Victor sighed.

"Jenny and me, we got separated. I don't know where she is. All my supplies and gear. Down into that trash monster. I barely made it to shore. I've been walking since."

"Have you seen the compound?" I asked. "Chimney stacks. That's where our friends are."

Emmy Banks shook her head and pointed grimly in the direction of a sloping hillside. "There's this amusement park thing that way." Her voice trembled. "It looks evil. Pure evil. I wanted to get as far away from it as possible."

"We're looking for our friends Liz and Kevin. Liz is about this tall, shaved head. Kevin is, well, he's a monster."

Emmy's trembling hand covered her mouth.

"You're kids," she whispered.

She looked at me as if she were truly seeing me for the first time. With this realization came a sudden look of fear on her face.

"I'm going to be fourteen in two months," Curtis said.

"I followed your orders to this island," Emmy gasped. "And you're just some kid. Where's the order? Where's the council? Where's the rest of the rescue party?"

"We're the start of it," I said.

"My goodness. We're not going to make it off this island alive," Emmy whispered. "I'm going to die because I listened to a bunch of kids."

"That's maybe a little offensive," I said. "We've done this kind of thing before."

"Twice, actually," said Berna.

A sudden rush of air. Branches snapped in the gust of powerful wings. Talons dove and snatched Emmy Banks by her shoulders.

Within seconds, Emmy Banks was in the air, screaming. She grabbed tree branches as the gargoyle's wings furiously beat the air.

Curtis aimed his crossbow. Bowstring taught. Squinting carefully.

His arrow slashed the sky and missed the beast's wing. The flying terror's gray eyes studied our faces. It emitted a high-pitched squeal and flew out of range with its shrieking prey.

The hairs on the back of my neck prickled up from a strong rush of wind.

"Run!" I screamed.

The treetops exploded. With piercing squeals, two

gargoyles dove after us. We ran, darting over rocks and roots. Their toothy jaws snapped behind us. Talons slashed. They hovered a few feet off the ground, expertly weaving around tree trunks.

Curtis loaded another arrow and haphazardly fired backward. It whizzed past Victor's face, missing his ear.

"Watch it!" screamed Victor.

Cassie tripped and slammed into the dirt, the sitter sat-phone skidding away through the dead leaves. Berna grabbed for her as reptile-like claws ripped into Cassie's backpack, and suddenly, Cassie was in the air, flailing in the gargoyle's grip.

Curtis dropped his crossbow and grabbed Cassie's legs. But the gargoyle was too strong. Curtis was lifted up. I jumped and grabbed Curtis's legs and held on tight. The tips of my toes skidded across the forest floor, and then I was in the air, too.

"Help!" I screamed.

Victor's arms clamped around my legs. Wind from the monster's wings kicked up a blizzard of dead leaves. The gargoyle refused to release Cassie's backpack from its grip. I looked down and saw Victor's wide-eyed fear. His sneakers were barely touching the ground.

"Here comes the other one!" Curtis screamed.

The third gargoyle dipped into a sharp U-turn in

the sky and sailed toward us. We were defenseless, wide-open targets. Kids in a barrel.

The approaching gargoyle's maw opened unnaturally wide. Its jagged nails stretched out hungrily. It was coming in for the kill.

A whistling blur shot past. An arrow pierced its veiny wing. The monster squealed and barrel-rolled past us and slammed into a tree. Wood exploded, and the gargoyle smashed face-first into the forest floor.

We looked where the arrow had come from and saw Berna, reloading the crossbow.

"Nice one, Berna!" I cried.

Berna fumbled to pull back the bowstring. The gargoyle was dragging all of us through the air to a deep gorge. I suddenly remembered watching seagulls eat clams on the beach when I was a little kid. The seagulls had lifted the clams high into the sky and then dropped them onto the rocks, breaking the clamshells into a gooey mess. In this case, we were the clams.

Click-clack! Berna snapped the crossbow string into place and loaded an arrow.

"Stay still," Berna said.

"Little difficult!" I said.

I know she was aiming at the gargoyle holding on to Cassie, but it sure seemed like she was going to shoot one of us.

"Left! To the left!" Victor cried.

"No, the right!" Curtis screamed.

"Don't shoot!" Cassie shrieked.

"Shoot!" I shouted.

Berna squinted and took aim. I closed my eyes.

The arrow shot past my face and whiffed into the treetops.

An inch more to the right, and my nose would have been the bull's-eye.

The relentless gargoyle towed us to the edge of a gorge. There was a slicing noise above me.

Cassie had cut through her backpack strap.

We fell like sacks of potatoes trying to do a cheerleader pyramid. The gargoyle vaulted into the sky with Cassie's backpack in its clutches. We tumbled off each other and sprang to our feet.

"Let him have it!" I screamed.

We hurled our weapons at the flying beastie.

Dinged with bumps and bruises, the gargoyle tucked Cassie's backpack under its tail and swooped off into the northern sky.

"My backpack! All my shtuff wash in there!" Cassie said.

Curtis scooped up the sitter sat-phone from the ground and tossed it to Cassie.

"Least they didn't get this."

I watched the skies.

"Poor Emmy," I said. "Looks like they took her that way."

"Add her to the list of people to be rescued," Berna said.

"We need to keep moving before they inform the Baron," I said.

"Shtill no shignal!" Cassie said.

The joyous sound of laughter and carnival music grew louder as we prowled up the sloping hillside Emmy Banks had pointed out to us. The wind whistled, carrying the smell of cotton candy and popcorn. A high chain-link fence topped with three layers of barbed wire stretched across the overgrown forest. A line of crows perched on the very top of the border surrounding the wicked heart of Sunshine Island: the amusement park.

A Ferris wheel slowly turned beside a winding roller coaster. A merry-go-round's organ chimed a sickly doot-doot-doot tune. There were booths with signs "Play a Game! Win a Prize!" Giant banners for the freak show tent advertised normal children. "The Girl Who Picks Her Nose! Come See the Boy Who Burps!" Signs read "No Parents! No Rules!" and "You Do NOT Have to be This Tall to Ride This Ride!"

There were twenty kids from ages five to ten in the park. They were screaming and running. But not from fear. They were having the time of their lives.

I watched one boy throw his friend off the merry-go-round. A little girl stormed into a game booth and grabbed a prize teddy bear and then proceeded to rip its stuffing out. A kid drove a bumper car off the rails and crashed it straight into a candy hut, causing an explosion of Skittles. Kids in the ice cream shop hurled scoops of ice cream at each other, like they were in a snowball fight.

There was a building called the Rage House, where kids with chain saws were chopping a couch in half. The kids giggled maniacally as couch fluff scattered the air. A tent with a DJ booth blasted angry electronic dance music. Kids in batting cages hit home runs into windows. A building made to look like a library was on fire. Kids danced around it, tearing books in half and tossing the pages into the giant bonfire.

"What is wrong with those kids?" Berna said.

"They're the bad kids," I said.

The babysitters nodded in agreement. We had enough experience to recognize a problem child—and this park was full of them.

163

"I'm not going anywhere near that park," Cassie said. "The lasht time I babyshat for kidsh like that, I ended up with bite marksh on my calf and a chunk of my hair cut off."

She showed us her scar. It was nasty.

"Ooh, they have a Skyscreamer? That ride's the best!" said Victor.

He was looking at the most horrific ride there, which was basically a giant slingshot made from bungee cords that launched the rider hundreds of feet into the air and then snapped them back down to Earth. I had seen people on YouTube going on rides like that. Just watching them get flung around was enough to make me want to throw up.

"Focus, Victor. We're here for the mission, not to go on the rides," said Curtis.

"I know that," Victor said defensively.

Furry-frog- and sunshine-costumed characters waddled around the park, giving balloons and prizes to kids. They were the same hunched-over characters I saw on the Baron's ship. Goblins in disguise.

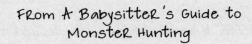

From A Babysitter's Guide to
Monster Hunting

NAME: Goblin

TYPE: Goblinoidus militum malus (note from Wugnot: distant relative to the far superior and more handsome species of hobgoblin)

HEIGHT: 3'—4'

WEIGHT: 60—90 lbs

LIKES: Cave dwelling, eating rats, wearing costumes, hiding, general foolishness

DISLIKES: Kale salad (or any salad, really). Being told what to do.

STRENGTHS: Scrawny, scrappy. Pack hunters. Strong in numbers.

WEAKNESSES: Malnourished bones and muscles make them easy to knock down. Individually weak.

BEWARE: If you think a goblin is alone, they are not. There are usually tons more of them hiding under the ground beneath your feet, waiting to overwhelm you.

The hunched characters seemed to be encouraging the kids to cause more chaos, applauding when they did something especially destructive.

Berna checked her watch. "Three hours until sundown. I really don't want to be here after dark. Better get moving."

I peered at the towering Ferris wheel. Every seat was empty.

"If I can get to the very top of that Ferris wheel, I bet the sat-phone will pick up a signal," I said. "Then I can radio Mama Vee for help. If I go solo, there's a good chance they won't catch me."

"But if you get in trouble, we can't help you," Berna said.

"Berna, it's my fault we're here. This is my responsibility."

"This is a stupid idea," Berna said. "And I like your ideas. I say we look for a better place to call for help."

"By then it will be sundown," I said. "The sooner I go, the sooner I come back."

Berna clenched her jaw. I could tell she hated my plan. Heck, *I* hated my plan. But I had to do it to save our butts.

"I'll go with," Victor said.

"You don't have to," I said.

"Babysitter Law Number Four: always take a buddy," Victor said. "Check the guide."

I smiled at him, impressed he had been studying.

While Berna and Victor kept watch, Curtis cut a small hole in the fence with his Rambo knife. Cassie zipped the sitter sat-phone into my backpack.

"We'll keep watch from here," Berna said. "Keep your walkie on."

"Thanks," I said.

167

I wanted to say so much more to them, but I didn't want to make a big deal out of going into certain doom. So I said a quick good-bye and crawled through the hole in the fence. Victor scurried into the tall grass beside me.

"Whatever you do, don't start making out," Curtis called after us.

Even though I was filled with terror, I blushed.

We snaked through the tall grass to the edge of the park, where we hid behind a busted whirly-seat ride called "Flying Aces." The chains holding the seats were thick with rust. Bolts and gears were scattered around it. A goblin wearing a dirty teddy bear costume stood at the control box, scratching his scalp.

A ten-year-old boy, with a candy apple in one hand and a funnel cake clutched in the other, ran up the ramp. The goblin quickly popped on his teddy bear head before the kid could see his real face.

The boy licked his sticky lips and shouted at the big fuzzy teddy bear. "I wanna go on this!"

The big fuzzy teddy bear gestured for the boy to get on. The little kid sat in his seat. The teddy bear pulled a lever. Gears clanked noisily as the seats slowly turned around in the air.

"Faster!" screamed the boy.

The teddy bear happily complied. I imagined the goblin's yellow teeth curling into a smile behind his teddy bear mask as he cranked up the speed.

From our hiding place Victor and I watched the boy whizz across the sky. His legs kicked with glee as he picked up speed.

"Faster!" the boy screamed again.

The chairs hanging from chains spun into a vertical blur. The boy's candy apple thumped to the ground. His funnel cake splattered into the teddy bear's face.

"Faster!"

Snap.

The boy launched across the park, clinging to his untethered seat. The broken chain trailed behind him as he rocketed into a striped tent like a cannon ball. The whole thing came crashing down in a billowing mess.

Every kid in the park froze.

They stared.

The boy staggered out from under the fallen tent and threw up his arms in victory.

The park cheered.

A jumbotron screen hanging in the center of the park replayed the insane accident/stunt over and over.

"These kids are loco," whispered Victor.

The giggling goblin removed his teddy bear head, snatched the dirt-covered candy apple from the ground, and ate it in two snarling bites.

Victor and I saw our chance. We grabbed the goblin from behind and pulled him into the tall grass. A quick thump from Victor's bat knocked the goblin unconscious. We yanked the teddy bear costume off the skinny monster's body. I yanked it on over my backpack, and Victor zipped me up. It was a tight fit, but it would do.

I plugged my walkie-talkie headset into my ear and pulled on the teddy bear head. I gagged. The inside of it was hot and damp with goblin spit and bits of old food.

"Barf level ten in here," I said into the walkie. "Smells like I'm wearing a bag of sweaty gym socks boiled in old french fries."

"You look great," Victor laughed.

Through the eyeholes I saw his amused expression. I was glad to see his dimple was out even if I was choking on stale goblin breath.

"Cover me," I said.

Victor hung back and kept a keen eye out for me. Wild screams and cackling laughter rang through the park. In a game booth, boys fired machine BB guns at tin targets. There was a video game tent where kids sat on beanbags, playing Overwatch and Minecraft. They looked feral. Like they had been playing for days.

They had no idea how much trouble they were in. Even though they were bad kids, they were still kids. They didn't deserve to be turned into monsters. I wanted to grab them and run them back to the babysitters, but what then? If I wanted to get everyone off the island safely, I needed to call Mama Vee and have her send in a rescue team.

Glancing back, I saw Victor give me the all clear sign. I was almost at the Ferris wheel when a goblin wearing a silly moose costume and handing out balloons to the kids cocked his head at me.

"Heads-up," Victor said over the walkie. "You've been spotted."

I swallowed and tried to stay calm.

"He's coming toward you." Victor's voice crackled. "Be cool."

Sweat poured down my face as the moose snout bumped into my teddy bear ear.

"Acka daka daka fun house," the goblin said in ragged gibberish.

The fun house? What happens in the fun house? I thought.

I looked across the park to the fun house, where little carts on tracks rode through a cartoon monster's wide, open mouth and vanished into a dark tunnel. Neon "Fun! Fun! Fun!" signs blinked and buzzed at the entrance.

Something told me the opposite of fun waited in that house.

I grunted to the goblin in the moose costume like *Okay, I'll get right on that.* I quickly hobbled off, before the goblin could smell me through my disgusting disguise.

The moose goblin kept his eyes on me.

To keep the ruse up, I approached a little girl in pigtails, who had broken into the cotton candy booth and was swirling her hand in the machine, covering her whole arm into a ball of pink sugar fluff.

I leaned down and whispered to her, "Hey, little girl. Whatever you do, don't go in the fun house."

"Ew! Don't tell me what to do!" shrieked the cotton candy fiend.

Jacked up on sugar, she kicked me in the shins. Ow! I winced and, to her delight, hobbled away. Glancing back, I saw the moose goblin had returned to handing out balloons.

"Nice work, Kelly," Victor said into my earpiece.

"Something's up with that fun house," I whispered.

"One thing at a time," Berna interjected over the line. "We need to get you on that Ferris wheel."

Scratching his butt through his smelly fuzzy frog costume, a goblin stood at the controls to the creaking Ferris wheel. I wanted to scale the side of the machine, but I was wearing a clunky bear outfit.

"I wonder what their policy is on goblins riding the rides?" Berna asked over the walkie.

"Boss probably doesn't want them to sit down on the job," I whispered.

Ding-a-ling!

"Kelly, on your six!" Victor shouted over the walkie. I spun around.

A goblin wearing a sad dog costume was barreling toward me, pushing an ice cream cart.

"Step back!" Victor yelled over the walkie-talkie.

I took a step back, and the ice cream cart roared past me. It smashed into the costumed goblin at the controls. He bounced and slammed down on his fuzzy frog face.

Every kid in the park cheered and laughed.

The jumbotron beamed an instant replay.

The dog goblin escorted me to the Ferris wheel controls. Through the dark screen over the costume's eyeholes, I could see Victor's handsome brown eyes.

"Nice work, Victor," I said.

While the kids and goblins ooohed at the jumbotron, I snuck up the ramp to the Ferris wheel. A seat swung down. I dove onto it.

My stomach lurched as I rose fifty feet into the air, sailing up, up, up the rickety old wheel.

I hunched down to keep from being spotted. My teddy bear paws were slippery against the plastic seat, and I almost tumbled to my death. The seat was loose and shaky. There was no safety bar.

I peered out at the vast horizon. From up here I could see a pair of train tracks trailing out of the back of the fun house. The cart rails zigzagged into the north, where the earth was scorched and dug up and dead. In the very distance I could see an enclosed prison-like compound where chimney stacks spewed toxic yellow mist over a gaping quarry.

The chimney stacks that were in Liz's picture! And that was in the direction where Emmy Banks was taken. They looked miles away, but at least I could finally see them.

The sitter sat-phone had no reception bars, but as the Ferris wheel reached its peak and lifted me out of the amusement park, two signal bars appeared. Yes! I dialed Mama Vee, but then as the Ferris wheel descended and I dove back into the amusement park, the bars disappeared.

"Victor, I'm going to need you to stop the Ferris wheel."

"Copy that," Victor said over the walkie.

I clutched the sitter sat-phone, waiting for the bars to reappear.

Then thankfully: two bright bars flashed.

"Now!"

The ride squealed horribly and jerked to a stop. The

wobbly seat toppled forward, almost spilling me out. I caught myself, the phone, and my breath. Carefully, very carefully, I sat back in the seat, hoping the ride didn't fall apart while I was sitting on it.

I took off my teddy bear head and dialed Mama Vee.

She answered.

"Kelly?" Mama Vee screamed. I could hear the fear in her voice. "Where are you?"

"We're okay," I said. "But we could use a hand."

"Is that them?" Wugnot's gruff voice bellowing in the background. "Give me the phone!"

"Kelly, why would you do this?" Vee asked.

She sounded desperate. I knew this was going to be bad, but I didn't realize exactly how awful. I looked at the fence, where I could see the flash of light off Berna's binoculars in the reeds.

"Are you safe?" Mama Vee asked.

"We're doing pretty well, except for the fact that we don't have a ride home," I said.

Vee sounded exasperated but focused. I could hear the sound of her picking up a pen. "Send me your coordinates. Me and Wugnot will find a boat."

"No boats!" I said. "The ocean around the island is protected by a trash gyre."

"Didn't they make a movie out of that in the eighties?"

176

"Yeah. But this one's way more real and superdeadly."

"Can you get us a helicopter?" Vee asked Wugnot.

"Not on such short notice. Unless you want to drive me down to the news station and borrow their traffic helicopter?"

"There's also gargoyles," I said.

"Gargoyles?" Wugnot said. "I hate gargoyles."

"Hold on. I'm patching in Elder Pressbury," Vee said.

"Do you have to?" I asked.

"Unfortunately," Mama Vee said.

The sun was setting into a bright orange ball. A cool wind shook the rusty Ferris wheel beams. Looking down, I saw a few of the spokes had come loose and were dangling like broken chopsticks. At the very bottom Victor was arguing with the cotton-candy-handed girl, who wanted to go on the Ferris wheel.

Click. The stern, crisp voice of Elder Pressbury came through.

"Miss Ferguson," she hissed.

"Elder Pressbury, I'll understand if you want to demote me or fine me, but we could really use your help since you have a plane."

"Well, I am glad I can be of service to you, Miss Ferguson."

Man, her sarcasm game is on point!

"We are in need of emergency extraction," I said.

"Speak up, dear. Didn't hear that," she shot back.

"The babysitters need to evacuate Sunshine Island."

"I see. I see." I imagined her cleaning her glasses. How could she be so calm at a time like this? "You thought it was better to ask for forgiveness than ask for permission. And we should come in and pick up the pieces because that's what we do, is it?"

I gulped. She was not letting me off the hook.

"Well, young lady, now you are in a prison of your own making. Because it will take us at least twenty-four hours to mobilize a team for extraction."

"Twenty-four hours?" I shouted. "We need a pickup now."

"Well, you should have thought of that before you broke the laws. They are there for a reason, you know."

My heart pounded. Wind stung my eyes. "Please don't punish my friends for something I did. I made them come here."

"They're old enough to know better," Pressbury sneered. "But clearly not old enough to survive on their own. The Nanny Brigade is cleaning up a crisis of elves in Washington, DC. Yours is not the only chapter protecting the children of the world, young lady. They can mobilize in the time I gave you. And in that time, you are to hide and *remain* hidden. Do not interact. Do not engage. Repeat, do not engage. For your own safety and ours."

My eyes scanned the park. "There's kids here. Twenty of them."

"The naughty ones," Pressbury said tightly. "Worst of the worst?"

"What's that got to do with anything?" I said.

"Now you understand what happens when you're naughty."

Holy cow. She is being a class A jerk.

"What are the coordinates?" she demanded.

I peered into the northern horizon where I could see the chimney stacks of the prison camp. My heart told me Liz and Kevin were out there fighting the good fight. Either way, I came here to find them. I was going to bring them home.

I checked the map and gave Pressbury directions to the western tip of the island. To get there we would have to cross by the compound and its chimney stacks.

If we're going to be stuck here for twenty-four hours, then I'm going to make the most of it.

"Very well," Pressbury said. "See you in twenty-four hours. Please do stay alive. And if you are caught, do not reveal our plans or your identity, or we will be forced to abandon the mission. Am I being clear?"

Grrrrr.

"Do you think you can follow orders this time? Because I will not mobilize the Nanny Brigade if you are inclined to disobey my orders yet again," said Pressbury with mocking weariness.

Yeah, lady, I heard you the first time.

"Yes. Ma'am," I said through my clenched teeth.

"Until tomorrow," she said.

She hung up. My heart had been stabbed with a thousand knives. The sun had gone down. The sky was a wistful, purple twilight. Strings of lights twinkled in the park. My insides were twisted into knots, and I didn't want the others to hear the pain and fear bubbling inside of me.

The others need me to be strong and tough and a leader.

I took a breath of cool air. A sound made me sit up in terror.

It was the shrieking of gargoyles.

Three winged monsters arced over the horizon and headed for the amusement park. Perched at the top of the Ferris wheel, I was a sitting duck. Sure, I was disguised in a stinky teddy bear costume, but that would probably draw more attention to me. Like *Who is that weirdo chilling alone on the top of a Ferris wheel?*

Clanging gears screeched into motion, and my seat began its slow descent to the ground. The flying sentinels swooped past the roller coaster, scanning the area. I saw a few kids look up into the sky with wonder. They pointed and yelled. The gargoyles shot high up and vanished into a cloud cluster.

I guessed the monsters of the island were not

supposed to reveal themselves to the kids. Maybe the Wolf wanted to catch them off guard.

My creaking seat scraped against a support beam as Victor stopped the ride. I hopped off at the bottom and a screw popped loose. My seat crashed to the ground.

The goblin in the frog costume stopped us. Apparently, he was the only one in the park who didn't appreciate Victor's ice cream cart stunt.

If that goblin signals the other monsters, we're in trouble.

I saw the goblin's yellow eyes widen with surprise. He knew we weren't goblins. Busted! I put up my hands, as if I were surrendering, but then I grabbed him by the green scruff of his frog costume and with all my might, slammed him into the Ferris wheel's metal support beam. He let out a weary grunt. I shoved him onto the next oncoming seat, Victor kicked the lever, and we watched the goblin sail up, up, up to the very top of the wheel. Victor cranked the ride to a stop, stranding the sleepy goblin in the sky.

We made our way across the park, and headed toward the Flying Aces ride, when the sound of trumpets erupted over the speaker system.

A brassy fanfare boomed. A smooth, royal-sounding voice echoed across the park.

"Attention, boys and girls! Are we having fun?" It was Baron von Eisenvult.

The kids cheered.

"I can't hear you!" said the voice.

The kids squealed with delight.

"Do you want to have even more fun?" asked the voice. "Well, then make your way to the most fun you will ever have in your entire life: the fun house!"

Spotlights swept the park and blasted the fun house entrance. The eyes of the cartoon monster face twisted and turned while a deep chuckle echoed from deep inside it. Costumed goblins were merrily leading all the kids in the park to sit inside of the rail carts.

Victor and I ducked behind the candy hut and watched the goblins lock safety harnesses over the kids' shoulders. This was the only ride in the park that seemed to have safety harnesses. I had a feeling they weren't there to protect the kids but to trap them.

"Keep your arms and legs inside the moving vehicle at all times. And please, no flash photography," boomed the Wolf. "Now get ready to scream. Because this is the ride of your lives!"

A goblin cranked the controls, and electric sparks shot from the wheels, sending the carts charging into the depths of the fun house. The goblins waved bye-bye. Kids screamed as they plunged into the darkness.

After they made sure each and every boy and girl in the park had boarded the ride, the goblins ripped off their fuzzy costumes and kicked them aside. The goblins scratched their warty skin. They each jumped into a cart and rode after the children.

And like that, the park was empty and eerily quiet.

25

"Let me get this straight. You want to go in the fun house, get on the ride, and follow it to Lord knows where?" Berna said.

"I know exactly where it goes," I said. "The chimney stacks. The compound. Where Liz and Kevin and the kids are."

We were hiding in the tall grass by the barbed-wire fence. The moon was out. It was dark. It was scary. And no one was excited about my plan.

"If Elder Preshbury shaid we should hide and wait, that'sh exactly what we should do," Cassie said.

"I'm with Cassie on this one," Berna said.

I looked to Curtis and Victor for a little backup.

Victor avoided eye contact. "Twenty-four hours is a long time to be running around this island, Kelly. I'd rather go away from the danger. Not into it."

"I don't know, Captain," Curtis said quietly as his eyes darted back and forth. "This island's freaking me out."

His camouflage makeup had rubbed off his face, leaving big dark streaks under his eyes, giving him a wild raccoon look.

"Bad energy here, man," Curtis whispered. "It's in the ground. It's in the leaves. In the dirt."

Curtis picked a clump of dirt and chewed it.

"Ew! Curtish, don't eat dirt," Cassie said.

"You can taste the bad vibes," he said, shoving a handful of grass into his mouth. "Taste it, Cassie."

"I don't want to!" Cassie said, recoiling.

"Taste it!" Curtis said.

"It'll get shtuck in my bracesh, Curtish! Shtop it!" Cassie said.

"What's wrong with you?" I said. "Why are you being weird?"

Curtis chewed a mouthful of grass, lost in thought.

"He's always weird," Berna whispered.

"But this is especially weird," Victor said.

Curtis slapped a mosquito on the back of his neck and stared at the squashed bug guts in his hand for a long time. Victor carefully scooted away from him.

"We should head for the extraction point," Victor whispered.

Things croaked and chirped in the woods. Distant branches snapped under the foot of some wild creature. Everyone huddled together in mutual terror.

I held out my hand.

"What are we?" I said.

"Is this a pep talk?" Berna asked.

"Just answer the question. What are we?"

"Kids?" Victor asked.

"Think legends. Think warriors," I said.

They grumbled. "Babysitters."

"I can't hear you!" I shouted.

"We really shouldn't raise our voices," Berna said.

"You're right. Got a little excited there," I whispered. "We're the good guys. Sure, we might be outnumbered and lost, but we're together and we're strong. If you want to stay here and hide and wait for the Wolf to hunt us down, then fine. But I'm not going down without a fight. Because that's not what babysitters do."

I marched off like a bold, brave leader until I realized none of them were following me.

"You're going to make me beg, aren't you?" I said.

"Yep," said Cassie.

"Please?" I begged. "I can't do this without you guys. Pretty please with whipped cream and chocolate sprinkles and a cherry on top?"

Berna sighed and got to her feet.

One by one, we entered the quiet park, keeping away from the blinking neon lights and the noisy arcade. I kept watching the stars, hoping the gargoyles had moved on. I lead everyone around the creaking roller coaster and darted to the fun house entrance.

Berna, Victor, and I sat in one of the wooden carts.

"Can I join you guysh?" Cassie asked us.

I thought for sure Cassie would want to sit beside Curtis in the dark, but looking behind us, I saw Curtis sitting solo in his own cart. He was sniffing the seat with a spaced-out look.

We squeezed together and made room for Cassie. I made sure Curtis was still in the cart behind us before I turned the lever on the control box to "Go."

Sparks erupted. The carts lurched forward.

"Look alive, Curtis!" I called. "Here we go."

The safety harnesses slammed down over our shoulders. The two metal bars felt like hands holding me down.

Smiling, robotic kids spun around in place as they sang the sickeningly happy Sunshine Island tune.

"With friends near, you'll be happy here!
Full of cheer, there is no fear."

The animatronic kids looked in desperate need of repair. Their movements were jerky, and some of them were missing eyeballs. Their rubber skins were cracked and faded.

The carts glided through a cheap set made to look like a happy forest. Cute-ish monster cutouts, adorable gargoyles with big baby eyes, goblins with sweet smiles

popped out from behind the fake trees.

"I am so glad we didn't pay to get in here," Berna whispered to me.

A painting of Baron von Eisenvult, looking like

some grandfatherly dog, rose into view, and the music shifted into an oompah-pah marching band song.

"With friends near, you'll be happy here.
Full of cheer, there is no fear.
So be a dear and look right here."

The ride shot us down a rainbow-colored tunnel that turned around and around to a dizzying effect. At the end of the trippy corridor a huge spiral disk turned in hypnotizing circles. The awful song grew louder and more insistent.

"It's so much fun to watch it turn,
See it spin and make you grin,
Watch it go, and then you'll know
All the fun's about to begin!"

Lights were flashing, blinding us. The music was so loud I couldn't think. The spiral at the end of the tunnel was growing bigger and bigger, like it was made of stretchy pizza dough. It drew me into a sleepy trance. Bubbles popped in my brain. I was reminded of the Grand Guignol's hypnotic eyes and how I fell under his spell and almost died.

I looked at Berna and the others. Their eyes were

blank. Their jaws were hanging open.

"Don't look at it!" I screamed.

I covered Berna's and Victor's eyes with my hands.

"Huh? What?" said Berna, blinking.

"Shut your eyes!" I said. "Cassie! Shut your eyes!"

I looked back at Curtis. In the pulsing colored light, I could see drool spilling down his lips. His head lolled to the side. And his eyes were radiant and fixed on the warping, spiraling circle. We screamed at him and waved our arms, but the music was too loud, the colors of the tunnel were too bright.

I knew I needed to get to Curtis, but the safety harness held me down. Together we pushed. The ride fought back until, finally, gears pinged and the safety harness lifted from my shoulders.

"Hold my sword," I said. "I'll be right back."

Famous last sword words.

I climbed to the edge of the cart, hoping I could jump the distance between me and Curtis. The sparking train tracks and the razor-sharp wheels shrieked below. I jumped and crash-landed into Curtis's cart.

As I waved my hands in front of his eyes, Cassie screamed. Their cart dove down a hidden tunnel right below the hypnotic spiral.

My hair blew back, and I held on to the edge of the cart as it tilted straight down.

We rocketed down the rails. My stomach went airborne. Was I floating out of the cart? I was! I hung on to my seat as we shot through a dark cave filled with squealing creatures. I ducked to avoid getting my head chopped off by jagged rocks.

Curtis had the same blank expression on his face the whole time. I kind of envied him for being so oblivious.

"I thought you said this goes to the compound!" Berna shouted back at me.

"It does!" I yelled.

Though I am beginning to wonder if I was wrong.

"This might be the long way there!" I screamed.

The rail carts went vertical. I pressed back into my seat. We were slowly climbing up a rock wall. The ride made that chilling *click-click-click* roller coasters make before they shoot you down another horrible drop.

As we slowly rose, I saw tiny crimson-skinned creatures with big ears and long needlelike noses clinging to the tracks. The little red beasts had on work gloves and leather aprons and were tightening screws to the rails.

I squinted at the mischievous-looking beings. With a pit in my stomach, I remembered seeing them in the *Babysitter's Guide to Monster Hunting*:

FROM A Babysitter's Guide to Monster Hunting

NAME: Gremlin Americanus, aka Flibbertigibbets

TYPE: Evil sprite, Class 5

HABITAT: Factories, car engines, airplane wings

STRENGTHS: Mechanics. Causing major malfunctions. (You don't want them on an airplane or around your computer.)

WEAKNESSES: Contrary to popular belief, sunlight and feeding them after midnight is no big deal. They have always been little devils (gremlins from Chinatown are different). These mischief monsters are relentless. But not to worry: the crashes and accidents and wrecks they cause end up wiping them out.

Now I desperately wanted my safety harness on. I kept trying to pull it down, but it wouldn't budge.

Suddenly, gravity took another vacation.

We raced downward at a million mph. The gremlins

cheered for us. My brain squished into my skull as the cart flew up a ginormous loop the loop. Shivering, I clung to the seat as we whooshed completely upside down.

In a blur, I saw a pack of giggling gremlins hanging on the rails. The little jerks jammed a wrench in the tracks, and my cart jolted to a stop and Curtis and I were stuck at the top of the loop.

My sweating hands gripped the safety harness as my feet dangled in the air. I saw Berna, Victor, and Cassie roar ahead in the cave.

Curtis and I were stuck at the peak of the loop the loop.

The gremlins high-fived one another and made taunting noises at us.

The howling winds at that height made my palms sweatier. My grip on the metal bars was slipping. "Curtis, help," I managed to say.

Snug in his own safety harness, Curtis held the same hypnotized glaze on his face.

"Fun," he said.

"Not fun, Curtis. Snap out of it!"

The little red devils jamming the wrench into the gears mocked my voice. They were loving the show.

I needed to reach the grappling hook and rope in the side of my backpack, but I didn't want to let go. My wrists burned and my fingers stiffened as I pulled myself up to the safety harness and laid across it, tee-tering on my belly. Not the most graceful position, but I needed my hands free. I unzipped my bag, pulled out the grappling hook, and swung it at the wrench, trying to knock it loose. But every time it got close, the red jerks swatted it away. I was getting angry. I threw the hook and knocked a gremlin off the rails into oblivion.

With threatening grumbles, the other tiny devil-sprites scrambled on top of the tracks toward me and Curtis. I had one more shot. Biting my lip, I swung the hook toward the jammed wrench.

Good news: it knocked the wrench loose.

Bad news: the cart shot down the loop.

My last thoughts as I fell off were *I thought that was going to turn out differently than it did*, and then, *AAAAAH!*

Then the grappling hook caught onto a metal rung. The rope tightened around my fist, and I arced through the air as Curtis and the cart zoomed off. I slammed into the side of the loop the loop, clutching the line. The gremlins merrily hacked away at the rope.

"Shoo! Get away!" I said.

That only made them happier.

I caught the track as the rope snapped. With a shaky grip, I quickly climbed down the loop the loop. Gremlins cursed me from above.

"Suck it!" I said.

I fished my staff out of my backpack. It would have to do since I'd given Berna my sword. A gremlin

197

dropped down on me, and I spun, smacking the little guy into the air like a mushy baseball.

A rain of nuts and bolts pelted me from above. When I glared up at the other gremlins, they pretended to be busy. I smirked. The little creeps were more scared of me than I was of them.

I tightened the straps on my backpack and followed the cart tracks deeper into the damp, cold cavern, where the rocks sparkled with strange flecks of green. When my eyes adjusted to the dark, I tried contacting Berna on the walkie-talkie, but there was no reception.

Follow the tracks, and eventually, you'll meet up with Berna and the others, I kept telling myself.

I tried to block out the horrible thoughts, the negative voices, the cruel criticisms.

Who are you kidding? You're not a leader. Look where you lead everyone.

I had done a pretty good job of keeping down the dark stuff inside me because I had my friends with me, and we gave each other strength and hope. I wanted to look like a leader, but now that I was alone, the floodgates opened.

Victor hates you. Berna used to want to be your friend, but now she sees that you're a loser, she's going to drop you and never talk to you again. If they're even alive. Cassie never liked you. Mama Vee will kick you out of the order. Your parents are

199

going to be furious. Not to mention Elder Press-
bury. You let down Liz and Kevin. Those kids. Those
parents who have given up hope for their children.
What a zero. You should have never been a babysit-
ter. No one likes you. Total mistake face. All those
comments on your Facebook page and Instagram
were right. You're nothing. Do the world a favor and
disappear.

"Stop!" I screamed, clutching at my head. "Do not let this island get to you."

My voice echoed down the tunnel, which had split into two different paths. One set of tracks went down each fork. I studied the two paths.

Which way did Berna and the others go?

The rail switch was set to the middle.

I knelt down and held the metal rails on the right, but there was no vibration. The left tracks trembled in my hand. I pressed my ear to the rail. There was a faint rumble.

With a tiny flicker of hope, I set off down the left tunnel. To keep the bad thoughts away, I whistled a little tune until I realized I was whistling the Sunshine Island theme song.

Don't let this island get to you.

Sharp white rocks hung from the cave ceiling like giant, dripping fangs. I walked on the tracks to avoid the pools of steaming, swirling minerals on the ground that filled the air with an unsettling heat.

I took a breath, but my lungs filled with the cave's rotten-egg stink. The smell was so bad that I almost fell off the end of the tracks.

I wobbled at the broken rail edges. A dark crevasse waited below. I could see stacks of broken carts piled up at the bottom. A fist seized my heart. I cried out for Berna and the others. The response was the lonely echo of my voice.

I tossed a green glow stick into the craggy pit. There was no movement among the skeletons of riders past.

Look on the bright side, I thought. *You might be lost, but at least they're not down here.*

And then worry began to set in, and with it came my mean voice.

There is no bright side, you moron. You're lost. You're a failure. A big, dumb, redheaded failure, and you deserve to wander around down here forever. You're a mistake, not a babysitter. You should have never joined the sitters.

I probably would have stood there for an hour, mentally ripping myself to shreds, if I hadn't heard laughter. Like a bunch of kids who were watching television. I followed the giddy noise to a rocky ledge where a shoddy wooden walkway had been built into the side of the cave. A bluish light flickered deep in the rocks.

Maybe it's a way out.

Maybe it's your death.

Either way, have fun!

I crept along the planks and peered inside the glowing, craggy chamber. I gasped. Nothing in the guide could prepare me for what I saw.

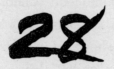

Ten computers sat on ten messy desks with ten hulking figures hunched over their keyboards. They were scrolling through Facebook feeds and YouTube videos and Instagram pictures.

"Check out at this loser with her cat," one of them said, staring at a picture of a little girl cuddling her tabby cat. "It's uglier than she is."

The others chuckled mildly.

From my hiding place, I couldn't see their faces; only their reflections on their computers. At first I just thought their screens were warped. Drawn by morbid curiosity, I quietly waded through the piles of potato chips, candy bars, power cables, and crushed cans of diet cherry Rocket Fuel Fizz to steal a look at these round mole people.

What I saw will haunt me to the day I die.

Their bodies were shrunken and withered into drooping sacks of pale, almost see-through flesh that hung down over the edges of their chairs. Their little legs had atrophied into footless nubs. From the sweaty haze and their rancid T-shirts, I took a wild guess that none of them had showered in years. Their arms, thin and wiry, were sunken into their sides. The only part of them that looked mobile was their twisted flippers that clacked away on their keyboards with remarkable speed. They were pruned into shriveled thirty-pound bodies.

Their eyes were bloodshot and swollen to the size of ostrich eggs, stranded in pools of drooping skin. Their hideous, transfixed gazes never left their screens as they swallowed the internet whole.

As the human beach balls scanned people's profiles, they called out their cruel comments while typing them:

"Nice pimples, freak!"

"What a disgusting family you have. Now I see where you get your bad looks."

"No wonder your boyfriend dumped you. Hashtag yucky girl."

"This one's superhot! Give her a billion likes!"

"Oh, yeah! Billions and billions and billions of likes! Hottie McTotty."

"Did you get your outfit from a dumpster? All you could afford? So sad!"

"Mistake face!"

"Ew! You are so poor!"

"You are a stupid fool with no IQ. Hashtag total life fail. LOL."

"Check out her bikini! So lit!"

They made each other giggle a little, but none of them seemed really happy with what they were doing. None of them ever looked at each other. They kept searching for a target, commenting, and searching again.

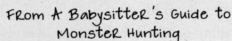

FRoM A Babysitter's Guide to Monster Hunting

NAME: Internet troll
TYPE: Mutated human
ORIGIN: Born online
STRENGTHS: Flaming insults, typing fast, hacking private accounts, bullying from afar, influencing people's

self-worth and perception of the facts by questioning and tearing everything to shreds. Disruption. Helping the enemy win. Ransoming people for Bitcoin.

WEAKNESSES: Human contact IRL. Showers. Power outages. Blue skies.

Gravel scraped under my sneaker.

"Intruder!" shrieked a troll.

There was a wet, squishing noise as they all turned to look at me. A troll lunged, but his squashy body was stuck to his seat.

"Message the guards!" one of them cried.

I dove for the power cord and yanked it out of the wall socket. Their computer screens died with a satisfying *voip*.

"No!" they shrieked.

Their slimy pseudopods trembled over their dead screens.

A meatball-shaped boy-troll angrily scooted his chair across the floor. "Plug that back in or we'll flame you."

I leveled my staff at his slimy forehead. "Only if you tell me how to get to the Baron's compound. Start talking, Meatball."

The bags of flesh sneered and looked me up and down.

"You're her," said Meatball. "The redheaded sitter."

They whispered my name. "It's Kelly."

I narrowed my eyes. *How did they know my name?*

"We know all about you, Kelly Ferguson. We've seen your pathetic posts and your wannabe pictures," said Meatball.

The others joined in.

"Your selfies suck. I can't even."

"She's the creepy Crimson Crusader! The Fire Face Freak! Ha-ha! LMFAO!"

My jaw hung open.

A weight sank my heart to the floor.

It was them.

The trolls.

"Your Insta-game is Insta-trash."

"Snapchat should ban you for life for the amount of times you've used the dog filter."

I slammed my staff into the ground. They trembled from the loud noise.

"Are you human?" I asked.

"Of course we are!" said Meatball.

"Aren't we gorgeous?" snickered another troll.

"Have you looked in the mirror lately?" I snapped.

"Oh, burn!" mocked Meatball. "Now who's being the meanie?"

I stopped myself.

Don't play their game. You might end up like them.

I know this sounds weird, but I felt bad for them. Once, they were normal kids, but something about this island and their addiction had changed them into monsters.

"Why are you doing this?" I asked.

"For the lolz," said Meatball. "It's fun."

My jaw clenched. "It's fun to tear people apart and make them feel horrible?"

"We also give out likes and shares."

"But usually that ends up being garbage, too."

"Even the people we make Insta-famous end up hating their lives because they feed on the image of happiness. But that's not really them, is it? Sad."

"Sad."

The trolls nodded happily. It made my lips curl into a snarl.

"Bullying kids from the comfort of your stinky chairs. You're a bunch of cowards."

Meatball proudly lifted his chin. "Hate the game not the player."

"But why me? I never did anything to you," I said.

"Why you? Because you were an easy target." His cruel, bulging eyes bored into me. "And because once the Baron sets his sights on you, there is no escape."

My ears perked up. "The Baron made you do this?"

"He knew he could tear you apart from the inside

out. Destroy your confidence. Ruin your self-image until you hate everything about yourself."

I swallowed hard.

Their mutated faces leered at me.

"And once we gutted you so you didn't know which way to turn or what to believe, you would no longer be a threat to monsters everywhere. You'd be a hollow shell of a girl, endlessly scrolling through her phone. Seeking happiness and approval that would always be beyond your reach. Clearly the Baron's plan worked. Because . . . here you are. A shadow of a girl. Broken, defeated. Stuck with the rest of us. Totally pwned."

A dark heaviness hung around my shoulders. My lower lip trembled.

"Are you going to cry?" Meatball asked happily.

"All the feels!" exclaimed a girl troll.

"Cry! Cry! Cry!" they chanted.

I wiped my tears with the back of my sleeve. "I'm not crying. Your smelly body odor and fart breaths are stinging my eyes!"

I sniffed a snot bubble back into my nose. Their cackles swirled around me. I closed my eyes to block them out, but suddenly, I was back in Willow Brook Middle School, standing at my locker. Deanna and the Princess Pack were laughing at me. The whole hallway of kids and teachers joked about my flaws, my weaknesses, my weird stuff. The giggles and snarks pricked like a thousand knives. And just when I was about to crumble under the crushing weight of it all, I saw through the laughing crowd . . .

Berna, Victor, Cassie, Curtis, Liz, and Kevin.

They were surrounding me, forming a force-field of friendship that blocked out all the cruel jokes and evil chuckles. I basked in their warm, strong light.

I opened my eyes.

"Go ahead. Laugh," I said. My voice was shaking. "If you want to make fun of me, say it to my face. I've got frizzy red hair and big ears. There isn't a name I haven't heard. Carrot Curls. Fire Face. Ginger Head."

The trolls giggled. They liked that one.

"I might not be pretty or popular or cool, but I know me and my friends are freaking beautiful."

They groaned.

"And yeah, I'm dorky and needy and awkward and weird, but that's just me. But you know what? I like me. So do my friends. So does my family."

Saying that out loud gave me a boost of strength.

"And if you want to say I'm chubby or I'm short or I'm stupid, go right ahead. Take your shot. But you don't know me just because you saw a few pictures and posts online. I'm not taking the clickbait anymore."

My voice was no longer shaking.

"I'm Kelly the Babysitter. And I came here to kick

monster butt. And that is exactly what I'm going to do."

The trolls stared at me in shock.

"Well, you're still ugly, so there," mumbled Meatball.

"Yeah! And your hair is so, so, so red!" said the girl troll. "It looks like your head's on fire."

I sighed and motioned for them to keep trying.

"And . . . and . . . and your face is weird!"

"Yeah! Mistake face. LOL!"

"You're the definition of the poop emoji!"

I rolled my eyes. "Guys, we've been through this. Now you can either help me find my way out of here and get back to my friends or . . ."

I swung my staff at Meatball's computer.

"No!" cried the troll.

I stopped my staff an inch away from his precious screen. The trolls shook like Jell-O in their seats.

Meatball whimpered and pointed to a crooked hole in the ceiling. "That's where the goblins come down to feed us once a day. It leads to the Professor's lab."

I cautiously looked up into the hole. A rusty, retractable ladder dangled from the dark opening.

"If your friends aren't there, they're probably in the jail cells."

I narrowed my eyes at Meatball. "You know your way around this place?"

"Like the back of my handlike object," he said, holding up his flipper. "Wait, what are you doing?"

"You're coming with me," I said, hoisting him out of his chair. "I need a guide, and it's the only way to make sure you're telling the truth."

Meatball flailed in my grip as I tied him to my backpack with a bunch of straps.

"Let go of me!" he cried.

He thrashed around, but he wasn't used to so much physical activity and wore himself out quickly. Panting, he resigned to being carried like a sad thirty-pound water balloon.

I dragged a desk under the ladder.

"Wait!" cried the other trolls. "You need to plug the power back in."

They desperately pointed at the extension cord a few feet away from their chairs.

"Why don't you guys take a break. Stay off-line for a little bit," I said.

"And do what?" they shouted.

As I scrambled up the ladder with Meatball in tow, the trolls yelled a flood of insults and cruel comments after me.

"We hate you, mistake face!"

The climb was long and hard, but I kept going, and soon, the voices below faded into nothingness.

At the top of the mile-high ladder, I shouldered a wooden door open and pulled myself and Meatball onto a concrete floor. I gulped for breath and rubbed my forearms. We were in a damp room filled with a wall of cages that held tiny monsters with tubes sticking out of their fur. Their blood was being drained into nearby test tubes.

I was about to set one of them free when it snapped a set of spiky, foaming fangs at me. I jumped back. Not only were they vicious, but they looked like they had monster rabies. Footsteps clomped around from the ceiling.

"Don't make a sound," I whispered over my shoulder to Meatball.

"You're the one making noise, bigfoot," he snapped. "I'm just hanging out."

"What's up there?" I whispered. "Hey, I'm talking to you."

"You said not to make a sound," he said.

I shot my elbow into his side. "Do not mess with me,

Meatball. I've iced monsters bigger and meaner than you."

"Testy, testy," he said. "Up there is Professor Gonzalo's creation station. But I wouldn't go that way if I were you."

I looked around. A spiral staircase was the only exit. "Is there another way out?"

"Nope. Hashtag you're doomed."

"Thanks for nothing, Meatball."

"Hashtag you're welcome for nothing."

"Stop hashtagging!"

"Stop calling me Meatball, neck beard!"

"Fine. What's your name?"

"Bow before the King Gamezee Seven Underscore Zero."

I cringed. "Your real name."

He thought for a moment and then said quietly, "You know, it's been so long since anyone's asked me that, I can't remember."

Even though he reeked of moldy cheese, I felt sorry for him.

"Well played," he sighed. "Hashtag Meatball sad."

"Look. You help me find my friends, and I'll set you up with a brand-new computer with the biggest screen and the fastest connection."

"And what do I get when the Baron kills you?"

"Dude. When I say I'm going to do something, I can

do it. I'm a babysitter."

Meatball let out a gurgling sigh. "Fine. Calm down. I'll help. Please stop talking."

A door creaked open. I slid under the staircase and held my breath as a goblin wearing a hairnet, a doctor's mask, and green scrubs bounded into the basement and collected the tubes full of black blood. The fuzzy, rabid creatures in cages barked and yapped at me.

I ducked down as the goblin's yellow eyes darted in my direction.

"Where's my fuzzblood?" a man's voice shrieked from above. "I need it yesterday!"

The goblin growled, corked the test tubes, and scrambled back up the stairs.

I recognized that high-pitched voice.

It was Professor Gonzalo. The mad scientist Boogeyman who transformed Kevin into an eight-foot-tall monster.

"Ooooh, you're in trouble now," Meatball whispered.

I reached back and whacked him with my sitter staff.

At the top of the spiral staircase, I cracked open the door and peered into Gonzalo's bizarre laboratory. It was like being in science class on another planet.

Professor Gonzalo was standing before bubbling

beakers and winding tubes filled with sparkling goo. He studied the black blood. His pointy goatee rose into a sweaty smile.

The Professor danced around his lab, plucking ingredients off his wall. He was surprisingly light on his feet as he sang to himself.

"A milligram of zombie warts.
Three milligrams of dire wolf tongue.
A quart of fire snake venom.
And one gram of rabid fuzzbug blood."

A puff of purple smoke wafted from the hideous concoction. It glowed pink, then blue, then red. The Professor drew the devilish mixture into the needle of a long syringe.

Seeing the needle made me woozy-wooze.

Sidebar: I freaking hate needles.

Ding! The timer of a microwave oven went off. The goblin assistant removed a stack of juicy cheeseburgers. The Professor meticulously injected the needle into each patty. The steaming burger meat plumped up and made weird growling sounds.

Professor Gonzalo sniffed his creation. "*Dee*licious."

The mad scientist whisked the monster burgers away on a silver platter. His goblin assistant pulled

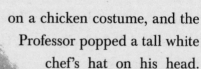

on a chicken costume, and the Professor popped a tall white chef's hat on his head. They vanished through a set of double doors.

"Dinner is served!" the Professor exclaimed.

A chorus of cheers erupted from the kids in the next room. They had no idea what they were about to really eat.

I snuck into the lab and tried to think of a plan.

The human beach ball strapped to my back smacked his lips in my ear. "I could eat those all day," he moaned.

I wiped Meatball's drool off my shoulder. "That's how they turn kids into monsters, isn't it?"

"Wow, Red. You cracked the case," said Meatball.

Stress crept up my scalp. I wanted to find Berna and the others, but I also wanted to save those kids from being turned into monsters. The only way I could do that was to take on Professor Gonzalo and his goblin. But that would mean giving up my hiding spot. I needed to stay stealth.

"This is a real pickle," I whispered.

"Mm, pickles," said Meatball.

What would Liz do? She'd go in there, guns blazing, with no regard for her own personal safety and most likely get caught and have to fight her way out. Okay, not an option. What would Mama Vee do? She'd say something cryptic and then wait for the rest of us to force her into action. Berna would chew gum and calculate the odds with her brilliant brain. Smart as I am, I am not a walking Wiki like her. So, what would I do? Good question, me. What would Kelly do? Kelly would do her homework and watch A Time of Roses and Cattle: Special Edition.

The lab had been filled with jars full of ingredients. Potions, powders. Firebird eggs. Spotted toadstools. Hobgoblin claws. Chupacabra venom. South American pixie wings. Death Beetle tongues.

I narrowed my eyes. A memory twitched.

I know these ingredients. I studied them for my concoctions and mixtures section on the Heck Weekend exam. Berna helped me study for it. We were on her living room carpet, and she was quizzing me. In my head I heard Berna read off the ingredients as she pointed them out in the guide.

I swung Meatball off my back with a thud and flipped open my notebook.

MONSTER CONCOCTIONS AND MIXTURES
"HOMUNCULUS FUNGUS"

This recipe for a living, sentient fungus is quick and easy.

    1 cup firebird egg, beaten

    2 hobgoblin claws, diced

    1 cup Chupacabra venom

    3 spotted toadstool caps and stems, minced

    4 South American pixie wings, whole

    2 Death Beetle tongues, crushed

Whisk egg and claws together for one minute. Combine with venom and toadstool and mix until it thickens to a gray paste. Add wings and tongues. Simmer over low heat and stand back.

Warning: use precise measurements ONLY as the fungus will grow a hundred times its size.

Darting around the lab, I swiped ingredients off the shelves and threw them into an electric mixer. So I didn't follow the recipe exactly like the guide instructed, but I didn't have time for exact measurements.

As the whole mess churned into a soupy slime, I listened to Professor Gonzalo's voice explaining the meal he had painstakingly prepared for the kids, as if he were a gourmet chef. The kids banged their forks and knives on the table, demanding cheeseburgers.

The mixer rattled and jumped. The purple goo ballooned out of the bowl and spilled onto the floor. Yellow and green spores bubbled across its surface as it inflated into a towering, purple sludge monster with eight slimy arms.

The top of its mushy head bumped into the ceiling. Its limbs puffed out and knocked over lab equipment. Glass shattered. Sparks erupted. The homunculus fungus expanded like a demented hot-air balloon.

"And people say I'm gross," said Meatball.

I grabbed Meatball and tucked behind the double doors. They flew open. The Professor and his goblin barged inside.

"My lab!" cried Professor Gonzalo.

I ducked into the next room while the Professor tried to contain the ever-expanding fungus destroying his lab. I locked the double doors behind me, trapping Gonzalo and his goblin inside.

The twenty bad kids from the amusement park were seated at a long table in a room drearily decorated like it was someone's birthday party. They were wearing colorful party hats and throwing confetti at each other.

"Who are you?" they asked.

"My name's Kelly. And I'm here to rescue you," I said.

"What's up, losers?" said Meatball.

The kids screamed and pointed at the troll strapped to my back.

"It's okay. He's with me," I said. "He's my tour guide."

"No I'm not. I'm an innocent guy who's been kidnapped. AMA!" said Meatball.

I snatched the platter of monster cheeseburgers from the table.

"Hey! That's our dinner!" screamed the kids.

"You can't eat these. They're bad for you."

"Are you vegan or something?" sneered a girl.

"I'll eat 'em," Meatball said.

The Professor's muffled screams shot from his lab. The green and yellow fungus seeped out from the cracks in the double doors.

"Kids, this park isn't what you think it is," I said. "We need to get out of here right now. Follow me."

I dumped the cheeseburgers in the trash, but a boy swiped one from the tray.

"Little boy, do not eat that," I said slowly.

"No one tells me what to do," the boy said, wagging his cheeseburger. "Not my parents. Not you. No one."

"He told you," chuckled Meatball.

I dove for the burger, but the boy defiantly shoved the whole thing into his mouth. I grabbed his cheeks and tried to fish it out, but the little brat bit my finger and swallowed. The kids watched in horror as I wrestled the boy and tried to give him the Heimlich maneuver.

"Stop it!" cried the kids. "You're hurting him!"

The kids ganged up on me. They pulled my hair and punched me to get me to let go.

"You're a horrible, mean person," said a girl. "You need to leave right now."

The twenty kids glared defiantly at me. The kid who scarfed down the cheeseburger stuck out his tongue at me.

"Fail video," mumbled Meatball.

The hinges on the doors leading to the lab strained and buckled.

I held out my shaking hand. "Kids, I know you think I'm crazy, but you need to come with me."

"No way!" they said. "We were having fun until you showed up and dumped our dinner in the trash."

"I know you don't understand, but it's for your own good."

"You sound like my mother!"

That made me pause. I did sound like a mother. Suddenly, I understood all those times when she told me I couldn't do something and I didn't understand why.

I took a breath. "Let me start over. My name's Kelly. I'm a babysitter. I'm a good guy. Here's my business card."

I was interrupted by a painful burp that came from the boy who had eaten the cheeseburger.

The boy staggered around the room, clutching his stomach.

"I don't feel so good," he moaned.

Muscles twitched in his back, and he fell to his hands and knees. Hair slithered from his twisting, stretching body. Claws grew from his swelling fingers. Horns slowly emerged from his forehead. Tusks sprouted from his jaw.

"What's happening to me?" he moaned again.

His huge paws reached out for help from the other nineteen kids, but they screamed and stepped back against the wall.

"Totes gnarls," said Meatball.

I unhooked the troll from my back and approached the shivering, transforming boy.

"I want my mommy." The boy's voice was eerily deep and low.

I rubbed his furry back, trying to comfort him. "We'll get you to her."

The boy's eyes looked up at me. They glistened with fear, and suddenly, they clouded yellow and turned into catlike eyes.

"It's okay. This happened to one of my best friends. What's your name?"

"Hudson," he whispered.

"I'm going to take care of you, Hudson," I said.

"Mommy!" Hudson cried for his mother again, but it came out as a braying howl.

Wobbling to his feet, he stood seven feet tall. He tried to speak, but instead, he barked. Frustrated, Hudson thrashed and roared. I ducked his swinging apelike arms.

The other kids screamed. "Monster!"

"He's still Hudson," I corrected them.

Breath heaving, Hudson looked down at me. He appreciated that I understood what he was going through. I gently took his paw.

"I'm going to help you, Hudson. But I need you to stay calm and do what I say."

Hudson wailed.

I held Hudson's paw and looked at the nineteen kids to show them that the monster on the outside was still a boy on the inside.

"I'm going to get you out of here. Are you guys with me?" I asked the kids.

The doors burst open. Waves of homunculus fungus flopped out with Professor Gonzalo and his goblin assistant floating and flailing in its growing jelly tentacles. Through the layers of goo, the Professor glared at me with surprised recognition.

He tore a hole in the fungus and shouted through it. "Guards!"

The nineteen stunned kids looked from him to me.

They nodded in unison. They were with me.

I scooped up Meatball and, holding Hudson's paw, led the children out as the giant fungus exploded into the birthday party room.

We rushed down a hallway filled with arcade games and found the exit. It was locked. I kicked it, but it wouldn't budge. The corridor was filling up with the bulbous spore goo. In five seconds the homunculus fungus was going to swallow us all up.

I showed Hudson the locked door.

"There are perks to your condition," I said.

Hudson roared and knocked the door down.

We dashed out into the night. The shockingly cold, fresh air filled my lungs. The outside of the Professor's lab was painted to look like a happy Pizza Party Zone. The roof cracked and lifted under the swelling, rising homunculus fungus.

I might have overdone that recipe a little.

"We need to get these kids to the extraction point," I said.

"I have no idea what you're talking about," Meatball said.

I tried to contact Berna on my walkie-talkie. All I got was static.

Quickly looking around, I noticed that the fun house tracks ended nearby. In the distance I saw yellow mist pluming into the sky.

That's the smoke I saw coming from the chimney stacks. That's near the prison compound, which is where the extraction point is. Maybe that's where Berna and the others went.

A thick, thorny forest of scorched, dead vines and trees lay between us and the distant chimneys.

"Is there a shortcut to the chimney stacks, Meatball?"

"Only way I know is through those woods," said Meatball. "But you don't want to go through there."

I was about to ask why not when an alarm whooped. A spotlight from a distant watchtower swept the grounds.

A tremendous wolf howl sent shivers down my spine. The kids froze in terror. The island hushed eerily quiet. Every living thing grew still with fear.

"Aroooo!" cried the Baron.

The Wolf was hunting us.

31

"Hudson, you're the strongest one here, so I need you to give a few kids a piggyback ride, okay?" I said.

Monster Hudson nodded. The kids hesitated, but Hudson gently offered his horns for them to hold, and they hung tight for their monster ride. I said a prayer as I led everyone into the dead woods. Thorns bit into my skin as I hacked my staff through brittle, twisting vines. Thick mud splashed under our feet, slowing our steps.

"This is why I don't go outside," complained Meatball.

"Quiet," I whispered.

Behind us, flashlights danced through crackling

branches. Snarling hounds leaped into the dead woods. They were gaining on us. We needed to hide. Up ahead, half buried in the ground, was a giant, hollow tree that had fallen. The massive, partially buried log was a good hiding place for the moment.

The Wolf can smell people from a mile away. And between you, nineteen kids, a rancid troll, and a monster boy, your collective stink must be like a homing beacon to him.

I stopped. Mud squished beneath my sneakers. The forest floor was covered in it.

I suddenly remembered me reading to Victor one day at lunch. While I was reading the guide to him, I could feel his gaze on my cheek.

FROM A Babysitter's Guide to
Monster Hunting

HIDING, SHADOWING: Mud can blanket most smells. So long as there is sufficient mud to cover the entire scent, one could, in an emergency, hide beneath the muck.

I scooped up a handful and slapped it on my face. The kids looked at me like I was crazy until I explained it was the only way not to get caught.

They rolled in the mud. Meatball put up a fight as I smeared his face with glop. Covered in muck, we crawled into the shadows of the cavernous tree.

"Don't make a sound," I whispered to them.

Footsteps approached. Snouts snuffed the ground. The children's eyes darted fearfully around behind their mud masks. We huddled together, shivering in silence.

A pack of wild dogs, and goblins with flashlights, rushed past our hiding spot.

I dared a look out of a crack in the log and saw four giant wolf paws stomping into view. A huge, wet snout snuffed the ground. It was the Baron, stalking us on all fours.

The terrifying wolf stopped. His sharp claws clacked impatiently as he sniffed the air. The Wolf rose onto his hind legs and stood eight feet tall upright. He scanned the woods, pointy ears twitching.

He doesn't know we're here, I thought. *He's lost the scent.*

"Come out, come out, wherever you are," sang the Baron.

The kids shut their eyes tight. My heart slammed against my rib cage.

The Wolf snorted and slinked after his hounds.

I exhaled with relief. They were gone.

"They're over here!" cried Meatball.

I slapped my hand over the traitorous troll's mouth, but the little creep bit me.

"I found them!" called Meatball. "Over here!"

Paws slammed against the hollow log. The children screamed as the giant wolf leaned over and slowly smiled at us.

"There you are," said the Baron. "Snug as a bug in a rug."

I lunged, but his sword flashed in my face.

"I wouldn't do that," sneered the Wolf.

"Meatball, you jerk," I said through clenched teeth.

"You've been pwned," said Meatball.

"What did you think was going to happen, Kelly?" the Baron asked. "You were going to rescue this hideous troll, take him back to your world, and tra-la-la, he'd live happily ever after? Look at him. He is a wretch. A freak. A monster. No one in your world would ever want to be his friend. He belongs here. Here, he is home with the other outcasts."

Six pairs of gargoyle claws stabbed through the tree bark above our heads. They shrieked, and the log shook. Trapped, we were lifted into the air. The ground vanished below. I held the children close as we were flown into the sky.

We were dropped into a stone fortress that sat in the middle of a lake of bubbling black sludge. Inside, the prison was littered with broken toys and shredded coloring books. It was like day care at Alcatraz. Goblin guards snapped shackles on Hudson. They yanked his chain leash and led him farther into the dungeon. The nineteen kids were locked in a miserable prison cell. I was taken to a single cell scattered with old action figures. Guards tore off my backpack, searched me for weapons, and then slammed the bars shut with a clang.

Moonlight beamed through a small window. I pulled myself up and saw we were surrounded by reeking tar pits that smelled like garbage melting into boiling asphalt. Huge methane bubbles popped on its surface. Skeletons of monsters were trapped in the tar, reaching out their limbs, as if they'd gotten stuck trying to escape.

"Look who made it," a voice said.

Across the corridor, Liz casually sat in her cell.

"Liz! You're alive!" I said.

"Go team," Liz said.

She held her hand out through the bars for a long-distance high five.

"Where's Kevin?"

"With the other mutants. In the mine. Nice mud mask, by the way."

"Is your brother okay?"

"If by okay you mean chained and forced to dig up rocks for twenty hours a day in the mine, then yeah, he's okay."

The nineteen children's sobbing echoed through the day care–prison. They were relatively quiet for once. Exhausted and shocked into submission. They all looked much younger and very helpless. They were bad kids. But they were just kids. They didn't deserve to be locked up like this. A heavy feeling sank into my chest.

"Have you seen Berna and the others?" I asked.

"Nope. Just you."

"Well, I'm not one to say I told you so, but my plan was much better than yours," I said.

"The order approved a rescue operation?" Liz asked.

I raked my sleeve across my face, trying to wipe the soot and dirt from my cheeks.

"No. They shot us down. We came solo," I said.

That made Liz smile. "Check you out. Breaking the rules. Being bad. The student has become the teacher."

"They're coming here," I whispered. "The Nanny Brigade. They'll be here by sunset."

"Don't need 'em. I have a plan."

"That's the Liz I know and love!"

I pressed myself against the bars to listen to her conspiratorial whisper.

"See the guards at the end of the hall? I've been watching them. They take a five-minute break every six hours. That gives us a little window of time to pick our locks and make a run for it. Their next break is in one hour."

"Great. How do we pick the locks?" I said.

"That's why I need you. There's a broken action figure in the corner of your cell. See it?"

She pointed at a twisted little military man on my cell floor.

"It's an old school Military Man of Action toy from the seventies. There was a huge recall on them because they were made with a metal frame inside that kept poking kids in the eyes. We can use that to pick the lock. Throw it here."

I waited for the goblin guards to look away before I tossed the action figure to Liz. She caught it and smashed the toy against the stones. Liz picked out the metal frame from its plastic bits.

I beamed. Liz LeRue. My hero.

Excited, I looked at the nineteen kids. They were locked up now, but if Liz and I fought hard enough, we could get these kids to safety. Outside the dungeon, the sun was rising in the pale pink sky. A little bit of light shined on us.

"I wish we never came here," said a little girl in her

cell. "I want to go home."

"You are home," said a deep, smooth voice from the shadows.

Baron von Eisenvult marched down the corridor wearing a camouflage military outfit that shined with medals. A black beret sat tilted on his head.

"You've had your fun. You rode my rides. You ate my candy. You destroyed my property. Well, now it's time to pay your ticket to the park," the Baron said. "And it's going to cost you dearly."

"You lied to us!" cried a brave girl. "We didn't know this place was bad."

The Wolf's tail swished. "Didn't know this place was bad? Come, come, children. You know when you're being good and when you're being bad. And you were all being very bad. I didn't lie to you. You lied to yourself."

The shivering children fell silent.

"But you didn't care because you thought you weren't going to be caught. Well, guess what?" He clapped his paws together. "Now you're going to work in my mine."

"For how long?" asked a girl.

"Until I get what I want," the Wolf said rather dreamily.

An enchanted, strange look crossed over him. It was as if he were listening to music no one else could hear.

The Baron held up an old scroll with an image of a green jewel that had a light beaming out of it and showed it to the children.

"Get a good look, children! This is what you're digging for," said the Wolf. "Pretty, isn't it?"

"Why do you want it?" asked the little girl.

"Because I said so!" replied the Wolf. "Stop asking stupid questions."

I narrowed my eyes. I had seen that jewel in the guide. It wasn't on a test so I didn't remember all the details, but I had a memory of Cassie pointing out an ancient drawing of the jewel.

Why would a Boogeyperson go to such great lengths for some jewel? It had to be special.

"Liz," I whispered. "What is that?"

"Check the guide," she said.

"Don't be snarky."

"It's the Jewel of Orgog," Liz whispered. "It was lost in the babysitter rebellion that was fought on this island five hundred years ago. Legend says whoever holds the jewel, controls the Great Orgog."

My mouth fell open in shock.

The Great Orgog.

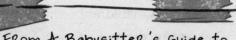

FRom A Babysitter's Guide to Monster Hunting

NAME: Orgog the Annihilator, Monster of Monsters

TYPE: Gigundo

HEIGHT: 350'. Maybe 400' with heels.

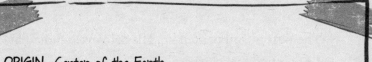

ORIGIN: Center of the Earth

AGE: Born before time began (whatever that means)

STRENGTHS: Destroying villages with one step. Eating dozens of people in one bite. Melting cities with breath of fire.

WEAKNESSES: Being sneaky. Always loses Hide-and-Seek.

LIKES: Sleeping for centuries. Long naps.

DISLIKES: Being woken up

NOTE: Orgog has not been seen for five hundred years (see Babysitter Rebellion). Rumors about a magic stone/diamond that controls the terrible giant have been around for years, but there is no evidence to support this claim.

The Wolf paced before the trapped kids. "Now, I know what you're thinking. 'I'm a child. I'm too weak and small to break rocks all day long.' And you are right. That's why the Professor will be paying each of you a visit very soon after he's tidied up his lab."

"No way I'm eating those burgers!" shouted a boy. "Not after what they did to Hudson."

The Wolf raked his claws across the iron bars.

"You eat them or I eat you."

The kids' frightened eyes bulged. The Wolf laughed so hard his tongue wagged.

"Leave them alone!" I shouted.

The Baron's tail perked up. His cold eyes studied me as he combed his whiskers.

"Kelly the Babysitter," he said, sauntering up to my cell. "Welcome to Sunshine Island."

"Miserable place," I said.

He chuckled and licked his chops. "Well, you won't have to endure it much longer. But I must say, after all you've done, I expected you to be taller. But you're a little girl."

"She's full of surprises," Liz said.

As he looked down his snout at me, his lip twitched. "I had a deal with the babysitters. They leave me alone. I leave them alone. But you've broken that deal and invaded my island. And now they will all be destroyed."

The Wolf shook his head in disgust. "If you had done as you were told, followed the rules, stayed home, shut up, and been normal, none of this would be happening."

I shook my head. "You were the one who broke the agreement. Taking more kids."

He gave a dismissive wave. "Bad kids no one wants. They're of better use here."

"To dig for your stupid Jewel of Orgog?"

"I'm the closest I've ever been to retrieving the jewel. I can sense it calling me louder every day. Why do you think I needed to go out and fetch more mutant

242

manpower? Monsters don't come out of exile for no reason, my lady. I needed that extra bit of workforce to retrieve the jewel. Soon it will be mine. And the world will know the destruction of Orgog."

Darkness crept over me.

That's what all this was for. To wake up Orgog. And crush humanity.

My palms sweated as I gripped the cage bars.

"It's like I've always said, darling: if you want to annihilate all of mankind, you need a really big monster to do it," said the Baron.

My heart sank as I imagined the nuclear bomb of monsters that would stomp my town to pieces.

"Why do you hate us so much?" I whispered.

"Because humans have taken everything I've ever loved in this world from us. From me," he growled. "My family. And now my beloved wife."

Of course. His ship's name was Serena's Song. *Serena the Spider Queen was his wife. And I destroyed her. I'd be upset, too.*

I gulped.

"And now I am going to take everything from you," he said darkly.

A goblin unlocked my cell and stepped aside. The Wolf unsheathed his sword. Cold sweat ran down my temples.

"What should I take first?" he said.

The shimmering blade hovered around my face.

"Your nose? Your ears? Your eyes?"

I held my breath as the steel tip pointed at my eye. My fingers twitched.

Wish I had my sword with me. Then this would be a fair fight.

"Or your friend?"

The Baron swung around and smiled at Liz.

"Are you that needy and lonely that you'll go to such lengths to rescue this worthless waste of a teenager?"

"She's worth a million of you," I said.

The Baron marched out, slammed the door shut, and approached Liz's cell.

"Point that thing somewhere else, dog breath," Liz said.

"You both deserve something wonderfully slow and horrible," said the Baron.

"I disagree," I mumbled.

"Guards!" bellowed the Wolf. "Take them both to the snake pit."

Snake pit? As in a pit full of snakes?

"Can't we just stay here?" I asked.

"Why, so you can wait for the guards to take their five-minute break, giving you enough time to pick your locks with your little toy and make a run for it?"

Liz and I paled. The Wolf's lips curled into a smile.

How did he know that?

"Do you think I got where I am by being stupid, darlings?" he snapped. "The only way you're getting out of here is through the digestive tract of a thousand poisonous snakes."

33

Hisses and the slap of slithering tails echoed from deep within a stone well.

Liz and I tried to fight back, but I was spent. My arms were frozen and weak. I wanted to sleep for days. The writhing pit of a thousand snakes below us wasn't exactly helping boost my morale either.

Six goblin guards bound us together with thick rope and then hooked us to a long chain dangling from the top of the well. The Wolf ordered his goblins to unspool the chain, lowering Liz and me toward a pool of twisting black snakes that waited a hundred feet below like a giant bowl of deadly spaghetti.

"Now this is what I call a party," laughed the Baron.

"If I ever see Meatball again, I'm going to grind him into bolognese," I grumbled.

"Thanks to you, that traitorous troll is happily behind his computer again. Now, let's see if you can shout as loud as the sitters from Maine did."

My blood froze. He had thrown Emmy and Jenny into this pit. Now we were next.

"How do we get out of this?" I asked over my shoulder.

"Hey, I came up with the prison break. This one's all you," said Liz.

Clank, clank, clank.

The chain dropped us closer to the twisting mass

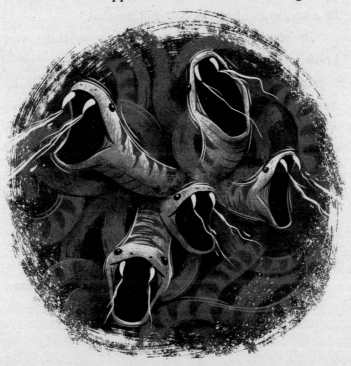

of fangs and scales. Snake heads reared up at us. Pink mouths opened wide and shot spurts of venom.

"Nice knowing you, Ferguson," Liz said.

"No way," I said. "We did not come this far to go out like this."

"It's a pretty cool way to go out if you ask me. Kind of legendary."

"Not for me. There's so much I want to do. I haven't even been to high school yet," I said. "I wanted to go to college and be a doctor and start my own company or write a book. Maybe even go to Mars one day."

"What are you talking about?" Liz said.

"I'm talking about not giving up, Liz. There's got to be a way out of here. You taught me that."

"Of course I did. I taught you everything you know."

"And Victor," I sighed. "We never got to go to the dance."

"Kevin likes you, you know. Don't tell him I said that. But we're about to die so I figure what the heck. If there's one person I'm cool with him dating, it would be you."

Clink!

We jerked to a sudden stop.

"Can't you see I'm busy?" the Baron said.

I craned my neck to look up. Three goblins covered

in black soot and wearing mining helmets showed the Baron pieces of rock. The Wolf's expression went from angry to very pleased.

"You've found it?" the Baron said. He inhaled deeply. "Yes. I can feel it."

Baron von Eisenvult peered down the well at us.

"Hello down there! I have to go see to my business, but I'll be right back to enjoy your slow and horrible deaths. So please don't go anywhere."

The Baron marched off with the mining goblins. Liz and I swayed like worms on a hook.

"Great. He's going fetch the Jewel of Orgog and destroy the world while we hang out," Liz said. "This sucks."

A memory sparked. I blinked.

"Sucks. Liz, your suction sneakers," I whispered. "You can climb us out of here. These stones are smooth enough. It might work."

Liz clicked her heels together. Her sneakers hummed to life, and the soles puckered. The battery readout on the side of her shoe was in the red.

"Batteries almost dead," Liz mumbled. "No batteries, no suction."

"It's our only chance."

I swung back and forth, rocking us closer to the side of the well. Liz stretched out her feet. The chain creaked as we swayed faster over the swarming snakes.

"Almost there; get ready," I whispered.

My feet kicked off the wall, shoving backward with all my might.

Thunk! Liz's shoes stuck.

Slowly, she began to climb up the stone wall, dragging me behind her. Liz grunted with each vacuumed step while I got a full view of the horrific crawling mass below.

Gibberish shouts came from above. The goblin guards had seen what we were up to.

Liz struggled and grunted. "This isn't easy, y'know. You're dead weight."

"I'd love to help, but my arms are literally tied."

There was a loud clank. The chain slackened past my view. The goblins had completely unspooled the chain. If we fell now, we fell into the pit.

Beep. Beep. Beep.

"Please tell me that's not your sneakers dying," I said.

Beep. Beep. Beep.

"What would you like me to tell you it is?" Liz said.

Beep. Beep. Beep.

We had another ten feet to climb but only five seconds of battery.

Goblins hurled spears down at us, trying to knock

us from the wall. Liz managed to scramble up to the very top.

Her sneaker batteries made a sad, sputtering noise. We fell backward.

Something snagged my ankles. Liz and I jerked to a stop. Hanging upside down, I saw Berna and Cassie holding my legs. My eyes lit up. The goblins snarled. Something smashed into them from behind. Guards tumbled past us into the writhing pit, revealing Victor wildly swinging his baseball bat.

"Curtish, give ush a hand!" Cassie yelled as she, Berna, and Victor slowly pulled us up. Curtis stood nearby, still in a trance, absently holding his crossbow.

They heaved Liz and me onto the floor. Cassie sliced our ropes, and we were free. I threw my arms around them and hugged my pals.

"How'd you find us?" I said.

"We stayed on the ride and got off before the pizza

parlor," Berna said quickly. "We camped out and waited for you. We hiked through the evil woods and saw you and the kids get taken here. So we waited for our chance."

"I freaking love you guys," I said.

"I love you too," said Victor.

Whoa.

"I mean, like a friend, not like we'll get married and have babies," Victor added.

Liz rolled her eyes. "You just had to bring lover boy, didn't you?"

Then the dungeon door swung open and a flood of armed goblins sprang inside.

Berna threw me my sword. A rush of energy shot up my arms. It was good to have a babysitter blade back. We fell into line and attacked the goblin horde, using their momentum to send them flying into the snake pit. Their shrieks were cut short by snapping fangs.

"Curtish, be usheful!" Cassie shouted.

Curtis blinked. Cassie pointed insistently at the goblins. He fired his crossbow and nailed one between the horns.

"Far out, man," Curtis said with a smile.

"What's wrong with him?" Liz said.

"The island'sh making him loopy," Cassie said.

We finished the guards, but more would be on the way.

Berna led us through the dark dungeon corridor. She had left tiny globs of bubble gum for us to follow like bread crumbs through a labyrinth. I found the backpacks the goblins had snatched.

"We spotted a dock where the Baron keeps his ship," Berna whispered. "There's other boats there too. We might be able to sail out of here."

"What about the trash thingy?" I said.

"If we're in one of the Baron's ships, it might think we're him and let us pass." She looked at her watch. "Extraction isn't for a while. Maybe ten hours, Kelly. It's a risk we have to take."

As usual, Berna was right.

With catlike silence Liz snuck behind the guards keeping watch over the nineteen kids. From the shadows the rest of us watched Liz creep up to the goblins.

The guards spun around. Liz knocked their heads together. The goblins dropped and she snagged their keys.

"Yes! Awesome!" shouted one of the kids.

Liz put her finger to her lips, instructing the kids to be quiet as she unlocked their cell. We kept careful watch as the nineteen kids silently padded out of their cells.

We helped the kids cross a narrow bridge over the smelly, primordial black ooze.

"Single file, boys and girls," I said. They listened.

Gargoyles shrieked across the dusky sky, swooping over the prison. The bridge wobbled and shook as dozens of goblins bounded from the jail behind us. Victor ushered the last kid in line to safety. He looked down at the giant, gas-filled bubbles burping from the tar pit that were spreading disgusting vapors into the air. Victor stood his ground. The gargoyles' wings pulled back, and their talons extended into dive formation.

"Everyone, stand back," Victor said.

He removed a bottle rocket from his pocket and lit the fuse. In a trail of sparks, the tiny rocket flew into a gas bubble and burst into flames. Fire ripped across the tar pit's surface. The shock wave sent us flying backward as the whole thing detonated in one big, fiery eruption that consumed the gargoyles and the goblins like marshmallows in a campfire.

We stared, stunned at the wall of churning black smoke. Then we all looked at Victor.

He smiled, shrugged. "I did my science project on methane gas vapors," Victor said. "Highly flammable."

"Now that's what I call babysitting," Liz said.

I high-fived Victor.

"Can we go home now, please?" said a little girl.

I looked at their nineteen faces. "Right," I said, tightening the straps on my backpack. "All of us."

35

I drew our exit strategy in the black dirt near the quarry.

"Boom. Boom. Boom," Curtis said quietly.

"Berna, Cassie, Victor, Curtis, you take the kids to the docks. Load them on the fastest-looking ship you can find. Liz and I will go to the mine, get Kevin and the others, and then meet up with you. If we're not at the docks in one hour, you take off."

"Ba-boom. Ba-boom. Ba-boom," Curtis said weirdly.

Everyone ignored him.

"No way we're leaving without you," said Berna.

"The Nanny Brigade's on their way. If we miss you, we'll link up with them," I said.

Curtis rhythmically beat his chest. "Ba-da-boom! Ba-da-boom!"

"Curtish, what ish your deal?" Cassie asked.

"Orgog is close," Curtis said dreamily.

"What are you shaying?" asked Cassie.

"Orgog the Annihilator?" Berna said.

Curtis put his hand to the ground. He rocked back and forth.

"He is rising," Curtis said ominously.

"What's an Orgog?" Victor asked.

"The ultimate monster weapon," I said. "He can level a town with his tail. Destroy a city with his breath."

"His scales are impervious to any bullet or bomb you can hurl at him," said Berna.

"And his hunger for human flesh knows no end," Curtis whispered.

Liz and I exchanged looks. "We better get moving," I said.

Berna grabbed my hand. I put my other hand on top of hers. Liz stacked her hands on ours. The others joined in. I looked around the circle at my friends. Our eyes were bright. Our hearts were full. Except for Curtis. He was on another planet.

"What are we?"

"Babysitters!"

"What you guys are is crazy," said one of the little girls.

The other kids giggled.

With a stern look, Berna faced the nineteen kids with the snap of a drill sergeant. "Atten-hut! Listen up, children. My name is Bernadette Vincent, and for the next few hours of your lives, I am your babysitter. From this point forward you do what I say, when I say. There will be no sass. There will be no back talk or pee breaks or goofy faces. Bad behavior will not be tolerated. No hair pulling, no snot-rockets, no fart jokes. If I hear one whine or whimper, you will be left behind. If you want to go home to your mommies and your daddies, you will be good, obedient boys and girls on your best behavior or the monsters will get you. Are we clear?"

The nineteen kids gulped. "Yes, Miss Vincent," they said, trembling.

Berna glanced at me and winked.

"That's more like it. Now, march!" she said.

Berna, Cassie, Victor, and Curtis led the nineteen kids north. Before disappearing, Victor looked back at me and blew me a kiss. My heart swung on a trapeze and did an aerial flip. I caught his flying kiss and tucked it into my pocket for safekeeping.

"Looks like it's just you and me again, newb," Liz said.

We fist-bumped and headed toward the chimney stacks.

The path soon ended in a quarry of black boulders

where an enormous hole the size of a football field had been carved into the ground. Liz and I hid behind towering piles of rocks and watched a horned, hairy mutant kid with shackles on its ankles trudge out of the mine to dump a bucket of rubble.

Liz and I crawled to the edge of the shadowy mine. My eyes strained to see down into the dark. On steep ridges spiraling into a deep abyss, fifty mutated, beasty-looking kids who could have been Kevin's monster cousins—chains around their legs, fur dirty with black soot—smashed pickaxes into the walls. Giant buckets of rocks were being hoisted up on ropes. Goblin guards wearing mining helmets with headlamps on them whipped the monsters when they slowed down. The monster kids said nothing. They didn't fight back. They worked mechanically without question. Their spirits had been broken long ago.

My hands balled into angry fists. "Not cool," I said. "Those kids over there outnumber the goblins three to one. If we free Kevin and the others, they can help us stop the Baron from getting the Jewel of Orgog. Sound good, Liz? Liz? Liz, where are you?"

Behind me, the sound of punches and kicks was followed by two goblins skidding across the gravel. Liz took their keys and their mining helmets. She tossed me one and smudged soot on her face. In the dark mine, with the steam and dust swirling around us and a blinding headlamp beaming into our enemy's eyes, I hoped it would be hard for them to tell us apart from the other goblins.

"I'm going to need a serious facial after all this," I said, smudging soot on my face.

We rode the clanking elevator down into the mine shaft, watching levels of miserable monster kids drift past.

"I can't tell which one's Kevin," Liz whispered.

"Then we'll have to free them all," I said, gripping my sword.

Farther down, the air thickened with heat and a putrid, acidic smell. It was like shoving a Sharpie up your nostrils. I wiped the sweat from my brow.

"You nervous, Red?" Liz asked.

"Me? Ha. Not at all," I said. "You?"

"Terrified."

I almost smiled.

"Thanks for being here," she said quietly.

I leaned my head down and gently clunked my mining helmet against hers.

"We got this," I said.

"That's what I dig about you, Ferguson. You got faith."

A howl echoed nearby. Liz and I perked up. We knew that howl well.

"Kevin," we said.

I stopped the elevator. Our helmet lights were dim in the choking haze as we carefully followed a narrow ridge. We passed monster kids breaking rocks. They cowered and bowed their heads obediently as we walked by. Our disguises worked.

At the end of the line, a goblin was berating a frightened beast and snapping the chain around its neck. The mutant kid had twisted horns and a familiar growl.

Kevin!

Liz tapped the goblin on the shoulder. He turned and got a face full of knuckles.

Blinded by our headlamps, Kevin fearfully put up his paws.

"Kev, it's us," Liz whispered.

Kevin blinked, then roared with joy. I shushed him. The last thing we needed was to draw attention to ourselves. His giant arms scooped me and Liz into a huge, warm hug.

"Good to see you, too," I said.

I have to admit, after all I had been through, that hug felt great. Then Kevin licked the side of my face, leaving a big wet streak of monster spit. Moment ruined.

"Toldja he likes you," Liz said, unlocking his shackles.

Kevin playfully shoved Liz and grumbled.

"Can we please focus?" I said. "Where's the Baron?"

Kevin gnashed his tusks and pointed down at the heavy fog that covered the very bottom of the pit. I could sense an ancient, evil pulse beating beneath the mist. This was the source of the island's weird energy. If we were going down there, we would need backup. Monster backup.

Kevin kept watch as Liz and I quietly went down the line, unlocking ten monster kids from their chains. They looked at their open cuffs, unsure what to do with their new freedom.

"We're babysitters," I whispered. "We're here to rescue you. But we need your help first. I know these monsters have made you think you're weak and small and no-good bad kids. But you're not. You're stronger and bigger and more powerful than them. You don't have to be scared of the goblins. But you do have to stand up for yourselves and your friends and your families and take your chance right now. Because you might not ever get one like this again. So join us. Fight back."

One by one their slumped shoulders pulled back and their spines stiffened. They stood tall.

A whip cracked and they instantly cowered.

A goblin marched over to them and demanded they keep digging. Kevin stepped forward, towering over the scrawny creep. The goblin raised his whip. Kevin's paw snatched the goblin's wrist, and he lifted him off his feet. The guard shrieked for help, but Kevin smashed him into the rock wall with a powerful squish.

Kevin let out a victorious howl, slamming his fists into his chest.

Everything fell silent. Pickaxes stopped. Shackled monsters looked up.

The ten monster kids joined Kevin and roared at the top of their lungs. Their voices shook the mine.

Liz and I stood in wonder as every chained beast wailed and cried in return.

Goblins raced at us with clubs and daggers. The monster kids bravely picked up huge rocks and hurtled them into the guards, knocking them down like bowling pins.

"I had a much quieter plan of escape in mind," I said. "But this will do."

I sliced a rope hoisting a big bucket of rubble, and it cascaded down on a pack of goblins climbing up our ledge.

Kevin grabbed the keys and scrambled up the wall to free the others. Chains broke. Cuffs fell. The revolution had begun.

Monster kids swarmed the mine, clobbering their goblin captors into mush.

Get to the Baron. Stop him from getting that jewel.

Liz and I climbed down a ladder into the murky fog. Kevin and three of his beastie buddies flanked us as we walked down a winding tunnel at the very bottom of the mine. One of the monster kids nudged me and smiled.

"Hudson?" I asked.

Monster Hudson nodded, happy to be recognized. He wanted to help. Though I was getting claustrophobic, it was good to have giant monster bodyguards watching our backs.

Liz held up her fist, and we stopped. An ethereal green light flickered around the rocky bend.

I could hear the Baron speaking excitedly. "Dig! Faster! It's almost free!"

"On three," Liz said, raising a pickax. "One."

Kevin and the monster kids extended their claws.

"Two."

I gripped my sword with both hands.

"Three!"

We bounded around the corner, expecting to be met by a small army of monsters. But it was Baron von Eisenvult and a single goblin with their backs to us. An emerald glow danced from the rocks they were facing.

"Baron von Eisenvult! By the Order of the Rhode Island Babysitters, I hereby demand you surrender," I said.

He didn't turn around. He didn't even reach for his sword.

"You're surrounded. Put your hands up and come with us," I said.

"Hey! We're talking to you, dog face!" Liz said. "Step away from the jewel and turn around, paws in the air."

The Baron put his hands up, and he slowly turned around. In his right paw, he held a glowing jade. Tendrils of eerie light swirled around it.

"Drop it!" I shouted.

"Orgog the Annihilator, Monster of Monsters, awaken from your slumber!" the Baron shouted with a deep and disturbing voice. "I summon your wrath."

A low rumble shook the cave. Pebbles rained down. I stumbled against the wall as the ground cracked open and wind shrieked from the dark depths.

"Rise, Orgog," the Wolf said into the widening chasm. "Under my command, rise!"

The earth crumbled beneath my feet. Kevin caught me and pulled me away from the the gigantic, gurgling gorge. Rocks continued to smash down around us. One more second down here and we'd be buried forever. We ran for our lives while the ground split.

Frantically climbing the spiral ledge, I dared a look back and saw something surging from below. At first I thought it was a massive pool of blue sludge, but as it broke through the ground, I saw it was the top of a gigantic monster's head.

36

As the mine collapsed around us, Liz jumped on her brother's back. Kevin threw me onto Hudson's shoulders. I clung to the monster kid's horns while he scaled the falling walls. All around us, the fifty monster kids hooted and scrambled out of the tumbling mine.

A blue-skinned behemoth slowly rose through the crashing rocks. He had a crown of scraggily horns the size of trees jutting from his head. His red eyes were as big as cars, and his mouth was a mass of twisting tentacles that looked like a giant squid was stuck to his face.

Orgog the Annihilator had arrived.

He hasn't even finished standing to his full height yet.

Baron von Eisenvult was proudly perched on the titan's shoulder, clinging to a set of spiky fins. The Wolf thrust out the jewel, commanding the giant to step forward. With a deep bass groan, the monster's legs plowed up through the ground. Chunks of earth cascaded from between the monster's school bus–sized claws.

Boom.

Orgog's every step shook the island. He was so tall, I could hardly see his head. He was like a walking sky-scraper.

"Behold the power of Orgog!" shouted the Baron.

Orgog opened his squid face. His scream sounded like a thousand honking geese. The monster kids shud-dered. Through the smoke, I saw the tip of the biggest, wartiest, ugliest tail I have ever seen thunder down toward us.

We scattered as the hundred-ton tail smashed down. The shock wave rolled through the earth, knocking us to the ground. I panted for breath, and as we wobbled to our feet, a shadow fell over us.

"Foot, foot, foot!" shouted Liz, pointing to the sky.

Orgog's foot blocked out the sun. We ran, and it crashed right behind us. This time I was ready for the tremor. It was like surfing on land.

"Good news is, Orgog's big and slow. We're small and fast," I said.

"Hurray for us," Liz said. "But what happens when— Foot, foot, foot, foot!"

We sprinted from Orgog's other lumbering foot before it splintered the ground.

"As I was saying," Liz said. "What happens when that thing gets to the mainland?"

"It could destroy all of Rhode Island just by sitting on it," I said.

"Tail!" Liz shouted.

"Do you mind?" I said. "We're trying to have a conversation down here!"

An arrow shot through the air and thunked into Orgog's ankle. A teddy bear bomb exploded between his toes. None of these things bothered the giant. If anything, they only tickled his feet.

Berna and Victor emerged from the woods.

"Looked like you could use some help," Berna said, reloading the crossbow.

Victor stared up in awe. *"Dios mío."*

"Where are the kids?" I asked.

"With Cassie and Curtis on a ship I found. It's a nice ship. It will make up for the one we lost," Victor said. "They're waiting for us."

"Foot!" Liz sighed.

A stampede of fifty monster kids followed us.

"We can't keep running. We have to take this thing down," Liz said.

Kevin growled bravely and grabbed hold of the creature's lumbering tail. The mob of monster kids followed his lead. Orgog stumbled, then swatted his tail and shook off Kevin and the mutants, sending them flying like a bad case of fleas.

"Nice try, bro," Liz said.

"Anybody got a nuclear missile in their pocket?" Victor said.

"The only way to stop Orgog is to get the jewel," I said. "Control the jewel, control the monster."

"But how do we get up there?" Berna asked.

Kevin grunted.

"Exactly. It would be like scaling a moving mountain that's trying to kill us," I said.

"We need a helicopter," Victor said.

"You got a helicopter, Ace?" Liz asked.

"I was just brainstorming," Victor said.

"We need a catapult," I said.

"Or a slingshot," Victor said.

"Where are we going to find a slingshot that big?" Berna asked.

My eyes narrowed with a horrible, terrible idea.

"The park," I said.

37

"We'll never get there in time," Berna said.

I whistled. "Yo, Hudson!"

Monster Hudson charged forward. I scrambled onto his furry shoulders and held on to his horns. Liz swung onto Kevin's back. Two monster kids bent down and helped Berna and Victor hop onto them.

"To the park!" I shouted.

Liz hooted like a cowboy as Kevin reared back and roared. The mutants shot off, galloping on all fours with powerful speed. Bobbling up and down, Berna and Victor clung to their monster rides. We thundered across the island. The ground streaked past. Wind rushed through my hair.

Leaving a wake of monumental devastation, Orgog

and the Baron followed slowly after us. I was counting on the Baron's desire for revenge to lure him into our trap.

We swept into the empty amusement park grounds and stopped before the looming Skyscreamer. I thanked Hudson and scrambled to the ride controls.

"Berna, we need to calculate the trajectory and timing to launch one of us through the air to land on Orgog's head," I said.

"Kelly, this is insane," Berna said.

"We don't have time for sane, Berna," I said. "That thing's head is the size of a McDonald's. You can land one of us on it."

Berna furiously chewed her bubble gum and studied the massive bungee-cord slingshot.

Just beyond the park, trees shattered. Berna licked her finger and felt the wind. Mumbling calculations to herself, she took measured steps across the park and then traced a big X on the dirt.

"If we can get it to stand right here while we launch the slingshot—given the wind speed, Orgog's speed and height—that should put whoever is stupid enough to go right on his head."

"I love it when you do that," I said.

The ground quaked.

Victor pointed. "Here he comes!"

"He's a giant, Victor. We can all see him. You don't need to shout," Liz said.

I sat in the Skyscreamer chair. I did not pull down the safety harness or buckle the seat belt, which felt really weird. My palms were sweating and shaking so bad I could hardly grip my sword.

"I can't let you go alone," Berna said.

"You need to work the controls," I said. "The rest of you get Orgog onto that spot."

Kevin wailed and gently touched my cheek.

"You're too heavy, Kevin," Berna said.

Kevin grumbled.

"What about me?" Victor said, stepping forward.

Berna looked him up and down and nodded. "Eighty, ninety pounds? Only if you're up for it, Victor."

Victor sat beside me. "You're lucky I actually like this ride," he said.

He held my shivering hand. Under normal circumstances I would have been totally embarrassed about him touching my clammy hand, but I didn't care. If this was going to work, we needed to be in sync.

Swallow those butterflies because a whole new flock is coming.

"Good luck, you two," Liz said.

She ran off with Kevin and the monster kids, waving her arms and screaming up at the giant.

"Crush them!" commanded the Baron.

Orgog smashed through the Ferris wheel like it was a stack of Lego bricks.

Berna blew a huge pink bubble while she flipped switches.

The ride hummed to life.

"Hang on," Berna said.

Clink, clink, clink. Victor and I lurched back in the seat. The bungee cords stretched in front of us.

"Feels like we're going to the moon," I said.

"Come and get us, you overgrown dog!" Liz shouted.

The Baron steered Orgog toward Liz and the taunting mutants. With each booming step, the titan approached the *X* mark.

With a final clunk the Skyscreamer seat locked into place. The long cords were tight and tense, pulled to their limit.

Berna's finger hovered over the red launch button.

"Wait for it," Berna said.

Every muscle in my body trembled with fear. I almost crushed Victor's fingers.

"Almost there," Berna said.

Victor was staring ahead, muttering a prayer.

I leaned over and kissed him on the cheek. He blinked.

"You're awesome," I said.

Our frightened eyes locked, and for a moment, the

world melted away and we were two kids on a carnival ride.

"Blast off!" Berna screamed.

The seat hurtled forward. The g-forces pinned us to our chair. I tried to scream, but my insides squished against my spine. Behind us, the bungee cords snapped. We shot out of our seats and hurled through the sky.

38

Through the tears blurring my eyes, I saw Orgog's tree-sized horns skewering the sky.

Everything became weightless and light. We were falling. No parachute. No net.

This might have been a bad idea.

Victor and I slammed into the colossal, wart-ridden scalp of Orgog. We skidded across the back of his head through a blanket of snow that I quickly realized with disgust was Orgog's enormous chunks of dandruff.

Ahead of me, Victor was barreling out of control.

"Too fast!" Victor screamed.

He careened across Orgog's vast noggin and vaulted off his thick brow, falling toward the monster's roaring, squid-y mouth.

I caught Victor's left arm. Braced my legs against forked horns for support. Victor hung over the tentacles of the snarling octopus beard. He looked up at me in thankful shock. Head lice the size of Chihuahuas swarmed up my legs.

"Behind you!" Victor cried.

A sword flashed down at me.

I rolled, dropped Victor, and grabbed my sword.

Clang! The Wolf's blade sparked against mine, an inch from my face. Foam seeped from the Baron's fangs.

I kicked the huge lice from my ankles. Saw Victor's fingers clutching Orgog's brow like it was the edge of a cliff.

"I'm going to eat you and your friends alive," snarled the Baron.

Our swords shrieked. He was heavy and strong.

"Why, Grandmother. What big eyes you have," he purred.

His weight crushed down on me.

"The better to see you with, my dear," he said in a grandmotherly voice.

He suddenly yelped like a coyote. Victor had pulled his furry gray and black tail. The Baron backhanded Victor. Sent him sailing through the air.

"No!" I screamed.

A slithering tentacle snapped around Victor's ankle, catching him in midair. It held him upside down over

Orgog's puckering mouth. Orgog was about to eat my crush.

"Victor!"

A powerful fire burned through me. Energy and anger vibrated up my back and into my arms. I chopped through a herd of head lice and ran toward the Wolf.

Our blades sang.

We fought across the rocking, tilting titan's head. The glow of the jewel beaming in the Baron's clenched paw caught my eyes.

"Why, Grandmother, what big ears you have!" he squealed.

We swashbuckled under giant horns. Orgog's head lice sprang at me. I kicked them as if they were sluggish soccer balls.

"You have talent. It's a shame to kill you," purred the Wolf.

Victor screamed. He hacked desperately at the slithering tentacles still coiling around his ankles.

Orgog threw back his head. I lost my footing; stumbled forward. I caught an antler branch, and my sword dropped from my grip and tumbled into Orgog's vicious tendrils.

My sword. My weapon. My hope. Gone.

The Wolf loomed over me, and his blade sliced a swath of my hair off.

"Get away from her!" Victor cried.

"You are not in a position to give orders, young man," the Wolf growled.

In the distance an airplane engine buzzed.

Pulsing propeller blades grew louder.

I looked toward the sound, and hope lifted my heart.

The DC-3 with the Nanny Brigade had arrived.

"Right on schedule," said the Wolf.

One by one, nanny paratroopers jumped from the plane and parachuted toward Orgog.

"Babysitters." The Wolf smiled. "So predictable."

The Baron gave his command. Victor swung wildly as the tentacles parted and Orgog's cavernous mouth widened. Bioluminescent blood coursed across the titan's tongue, lighting his tonsils up like a disco.

"Look out!" I screamed.

A guttural gushing gurgled from deep within the mountainous beast. Orgog projectile vomited oily blue fire. The paratrooper nannies' parachutes caught aflame, and they fell like shooting stars.

"No!" I screamed.

The Nanny Brigade slammed down on the giant's back and slid wildly down Orgog's spine. Their flaming parachutes tangled on the beast's dorsal fins. The paratroopers hung there like tassels on a cowboy's jacket.

"Again," commanded the Baron.

A blast of blue fire singed a wing of the babysitter plane. The aircraft sputtered and dipped from the sky. Orgog roared and swiped his claws at the circling plane. I saw Mama Vee and Wugnot watching me in awe from a portal window.

From far below us, I could hear Berna and the monster kids screaming as Orgog's enormous tail crashed around them. Across the giant's head, I saw Victor, upside down, about to be pulled apart, limb from limb by powerful tentacles, while my sword dangled uselessly in their suction cups. The whole time Victor's beautiful brown eyes were locked on mine.

"See the destruction you've caused? You fought nobly, but you have failed. You are finished, child. All of you," said the Wolf. "Your world is over. Mine is about to begin."

The DC-3 wobbled through the sky, trailing black smoke as Orgog's tail whooshed toward it.

The Baron kissed his golden sword's hilt. His eyes glowed in the green gemstone light.

"For you, my queen, Serena," the Wolf said.

My wrists trembled and ached. I was exhausted. Nothing in the tank. But there was a small flicker of light.

You know what you need to do, Kelly. It's going to hurt like heck. But it's the only way.

39

Eat sneaker, Baron!

I did the Swinging Monkey Sitter, kicking my legs up and springing like a jackhammer. My shoes cracked the Wolf's nose. I frantically grabbed his glowing emerald paw.

He snarled and sunk his fangs into my arm. His teeth pierced my skin. Flashing, blinding pain knifed through my flesh. My arm snapped, the bone breaking under the Baron's bite.

Don't pass out. You did this for a reason. Close combat.

I cried out. He shook me like a chew toy.

He thinks you're done for. He's lowered his defenses. Now's your chance. Grab it!

My free hand grabbed the Wolf's wagging tail. I yanked it like I was trying to start a lawn mower.

"Eeeeah!" the Baron yelped, and dropped my ragged arm from his mouth.

My blood dripped from his hideous fangs as his eyes flashed hungrily. "Blood of the babysitter. My favorite."

His tongue slurped across his messy snout. He wanted more.

"Why, Grandmother, what big teeth you have," he snarled.

I showed him the clump of fur in my fist. "I'm going to make a carpet out of you, Baron."

"Kelly!" Victor cried.

Victor had managed to pry my sword loose from the tentacles. He flung it to me.

I dove, my good arm reaching out.

"All the better to eat you with!" screamed the Baron.

The Baron lunged. I caught my sword. Gripped it tight. With every ounce of strength and breath I had, I spun wildly.

The Wolf gasped. He stared at his severed wrist.

His paw thumped down at my feet. Emerald light radiated in its grasp. I pried the jewel from his claws. It felt like reaching into a BBQ grill and grabbing a burning coal. Ethereal light swirled around my fist. Heat raced up my arm.

Unimaginable power surged in me. For a moment I forgot the sting of my broken arm tucked against my side. Monstrous noises and chants buzzed in my brain. I felt somehow connected to Orgog.

"Orgog the Annihilator, hear my command!" I shouted.

The giant slowed.

He was listening to me.

The jewel pulsed in my fist. The power put a wicked smile on my face.

"No, no, no!" the Baron shouted.

The Wolf sprang at me. I stood still and concentrated.

"Die!" the Baron screamed.

A flurry of tentacles snatched him in midair. Orgog's

squid-y feelers coiled around the Wolf, hoisting him over the giant's mouth.

The Baron whimpered like a scared puppy.

I looked at Victor. My crush was gently lowered to my side, as if the tentacles were the loving hands of a masseuse. The great Orgog made a happy, kissing noise. Because we were connected, Orgog the Almighty also had a crush on Victor.

I focused on the fiery airplane plummeting from the sky. Orgog's claws reached out and caught it. The gigundo beast gently cradled the DC-3 like it was a toy.

The startled faces of the Nanny Brigade, Mama Vee, and Wugnot stared back at me as I had Orgog set the plane down beside Liz, Berna, and Kevin.

Orgog carefully plucked the helpless Nanny Brigade paratroopers from his back.

Mama Vee, Wugnot, and Elder Pressbury stared up at us in wonderment.

"Miss Ferguson?" shrieked Elder Pressbury.

"Hi, Elder Pressbury!" I said. "Thanks for coming!"

Orgog and I waved hello.

Pressbury's jaw fell open.

"You have broken the peace treaty, you hag!" shouted Baron von Eisenvult.

Elder Pressbury adjusted her flight goggles and crossed her hands delicately.

"And we have evidence you infringed upon it, von Eisenvult," Elder Pressbury said.

Then the tiny old lady pointed up at me.

"Thanks to this young troublemaker," she said, smiling.

"You've started a war, babysitter!" howled the Wolf. "The others will bring a reign of fire and fear on your heads for what you've done to us. You think we Boogeymen are the only monsters in the world?"

I scowled at the Wolf, and Orgog shook him back and forth, shutting him up.

"I think when your buddies see that we beat the Big Bad Wolf, they'll be so scared they'll want to talk peace," I said. "And we seriously need to talk peace, because I have to get good grades in high school next year. If I'm out all the time, mopping the floor with you bozos, I won't have time to keep a three-point-nine average. Things need to change. This whole monsters killing humans and vice versa . . . It's stupid. So just chill."

"Chill, indeed!" shouted Elder Pressbury in agreement.

Swaying upside down by Orgog's feelers, the Big Bad Wolf gnashed his teeth.

"Never!" His eyes burned into me. "You cannot destroy us. We are evil. And evil is eternal. I will forever haunt you and every child like you. You merely sent the Grand Guignol to the Nothing World, darling. He could reappear in a child's nightmare at any time."

I gulped.

Did not know that.

"And my Serena? She's merely in a death cocoon. She could return as a twelve-foot-wide butterfly vampire!"

Eesh. Also news to me.

"One day, no matter how old you are, one of us will find you and we will kill you. We will forever haunt you and your children's children's children. I promise you that. You think you're going to change the world? Grow up! You can't. Evil is eternal. You're only confident because you're holding that jewel. Without it or your friends, you are nothing. Weak, small. Zero."

I inhaled sharply. Air rushed into Orgog's lungs.

"You can't tear me or my friends down anymore. We might be kids. But we can change the world," I said.

I held up my green glowing fist. "We have the power now," I said.

Orgog's humungous mouth opened.

"Good-bye, Baron," I said.

Tentacles swung the Baron down Orgog's gullet.

The squid mouth slammed shut, and a horrible howl cried from inside Orgog's crushing maw. It was a gut-wrenching sound, like a riot in a dog pound.

I burped. Orgog belched blue fire.

The giant bowed down and knelt before the Nanny Brigade and the babysitters. Victor and I slid off Orgog's forehead and stood on solid ground.

"Yeah, Ferguson!" Liz yelled.

"Babysitters rule!" screamed Berna.

The monster kids howled in unison and sounded like a hundred victory trombones.

Berna and Liz and Kevin embraced us tight. I winced. Blood soaked my right sleeve.

"Medic!" shouted Victor.

A nanny medic hustled to my side with a first aid kit. I clenched my jaw in pain as they cleaned the Wolf bites and put my arm in a sling.

"Yep. That's definitely broken," I hissed.

"Hope you don't turn into a werewolf now," Victor joked.

"Dude, that's not funny," Berna said. She looked me up and down with concern. "I'll need to run some tests."

Mama Vee rushed up to me. She was breathless. "Kelly, you guys. You made it," she said, holding me by the shoulders. "I tried to get them to mobilize sooner."

"We lost contact with the Maine crew," Wugnot said. "I was hoping they'd find you."

I thought of Emmy Banks being lifted away by a gargoyle.

"Emmy and Jenny didn't make it," I said.

Seeing our saddened expressions, the sitters realized Emmy and Jenny had come to our rescue and had given their lives to help us. And now they were gone.

"We'll give them a hero's funeral," Wugnot said, removing his trucker hat.

The green gemstone glowed in my hand. It sparkled in Vee's eye.

"The jewel of Orgog," she said, reaching for the radiant power stone. "On the bright side it's more beautiful than I ever imagined. May I? I've always wanted a jade like that."

Wugnot's tail blocked her from the sparkling gem. "I don't think that's a good idea, Vee."

Mama Vee snapped out of it. She blinked. Wiped her forehead. "Whoa! What's wrong with me? We have to get off this island."

Elder Pressbury walked among the mutant monster kids. At her side a nanny held a clipboard with a missing children list, and their photographs.

"Fiona Dubowski?" Elder Pressbury called out.

From the pack, a chestnut brown paw slowly raised.

The nanny checked the monster kid's name off the list.

Elder Pressbury studied the furry beast boys and girls. Her eyes glistened. "You're going home."

The creatures grunted happily and circled Pressbury.

Her icy facade dropped, and she kindly patted their shoulders.

"You poor, poor dears. I am sorry I did not act sooner," said Pressbury. "This way, boys and girls. The nannies will see to you and help reunite you with your families."

I saw Kevin watching me through the crowd. Our eyes met, and he jumped to my side. He sadly pointed at my broken arm in its sling.

"I'll live, Kevin," I said. "You okay?"

Kevin nodded. He gently brushed the hair from my face. He touched the swath of hair the Baron had chopped off.

"I needed a haircut anyway," I said with a shrug.

I pulled at his black and brown beard.

"You need one too," I said.

Kevin grunted and pointed to his heart and then to my heart. I knew it meant he was happy I was alive and how much he cared for me.

Victor's eyebrows crinkled. "What is he saying?"

"He says thank you, Victor," I said. "For being so brave."

We led the small army to the island's creaking docks. Cassie and Curtis were waiting for us on the bow of a two-hundred-foot yacht that looked like it belonged to a tech billionaire.

"Hey, you guysh!" said Cassie, waving at us.

The nineteen boys and girls rushed to the edge of the deck, waving and screaming happily.

The Nanny Brigade stared up in amazement.

"Do wonders never cease?" Mama Vee whispered.

Cassie bounded down the gangplank. "I can't believe I freaking misshed the whole thing! Ack! I shaw shome of it from here—that thing wash huge! Curtish is shtill all weird. I didn't want to leave him alone with theesh rugratsh. I shwear, I do not know what I shee in that boy."

"You didn't die," said Curtis in a spaced-out voice. "Groovy."

"Who even shaysh 'groovy'? We need to get you off thish island."

Elder Pressbury hobbled over and took us in.

"Berna. Victor. The LeRue siblings. Cassie. Curtis. And Miss Ferguson," she said through her wrinkled, pursed lips.

"You lot are the worst babysitters I have ever encountered! You're rude. You're naughty. Full of mischief. You don't follow orders. You're bad. Rotten to the core. Your actions are unacceptable. You broke every rule and law of this great order, and I hope you've learned your lesson!"

She stomped her fake leg, punctuating her point.

"However, you did what we were too scared to do ourselves. In fear of change, I suppose. Fear of failure.

Perhaps the council has grown a little old and a little too wise. A little too careful. Set in our ways. And it took a bad kid with a good heart to show us that nothing is impossible. Not even saving the world. Kelly Ferguson, you are a hero."

I shook my head and looked at Berna, Victor, Liz, Kevin, Cassie, and Curtis.

"My friends are the real heroes, Elder Pressbury. Not me. Without them we'd be goners. We won because they risked everything and they gave everything."

My friends' eyes glistened with pride. Elder Pressbury nodded in agreement.

Then she did something I never thought I would see: she smiled.

"Then perhaps it was we who have learned the lesson," Pressbury said. "Sometimes it takes a bad kid to do a good thing."

I had Orgog perform one final task: scooping the trash monster out of the ocean surrounding the island. The gyre writhed in the titan's grip like a garbage boa constrictor. Orgog dug up the collapsed mine and dropped the gyre inside. He kicked hills of rubble over the swirling plastic mush and patted tons and tons of rocks over it, as if he were potting flowers in a garden.

"Thanks for your help, Orgog," I said. "You can go back to sleep now. For, like, thousands and thousands of years. Forever. How about you have a nice, long eternal sleep, and if you need anything, call us. Okay? We're friends now. You and me. We have a bond, right?

And you promise not to destroy mankind?"

Orgog's enormous tail whooshed over my head and gently curled down so I could shake one of his spikes.

"Good night, big guy," I said.

The giant monster waved and sauntered off, leaving a path of destruction behind him.

I placed the sparkling jewel in a supernatural diaper bag that Elder Pressbury handed me. She locked the zipper and slung the satchel over her shoulder.

"I'll take this back to London, thank you very much," said Elder Pressbury. "Oxford has been requesting ancient monster minerals to study, and this should suffice."

Nannies in white hazmat suits swept the island. They found Professor Gonzalo and his goblin assistant trapped in the purple homunculus fungus. They locked the madman inside of a crate and hauled him into the airplane.

"Let me go, you bunch of losers!" a familiar throaty voice shouted.

More nannies in hazmat suits carried Meatball and the other trolls onto the airplane.

"We found them hiding in the Baron's castle, trying to get onto the Wi-Fi," said a babysitter in a hazmat suit.

"Hashtag worse rescue mission ever. Kelly Ferguson is a total Mary Sue dot com. Babysitters are evil. Don't

293

forget to like and share. And click here to subscribe," said Meatball.

The babysitters looked truly disturbed by the insulting human beach ball.

Elder Pressbury gently patted Meatball's head. "Come along, young man."

On our way home we all watched from the deck of the sleek yacht as Orgog waded into the ocean. The nineteen human boys and girls and all the monster kids waved good-bye to the ancient gigundo.

I peered across the ship's bow, blanket pulled over my shoulders. Berna sat beside me, and I held out a wing of blanket for her. She curled under it.

"Your math skills saved my life, Bern," I said.

"Do me a favor and tell that to my mom," Berna said.

"I'm sorry we fought," I said. "That was my least favorite part of the whole mission. Aside from the part when I was lowered into a pit of snakes."

"It's okay. Friends can disagree and still be friends," she said.

"Best friends?" I asked.

"The best," she said.

I beamed. Victor sat next to us.

"There he is!" Berna said. "Victor, I have to tell you, at first I didn't know if you were for real. But you're a good babysitter. I'm nominating you to take your Heck Weekend exams."

Victor's dimple appeared. Berna high-fived him.

"Think your uncle will be happy if you bring this yacht back to him instead of his fishing boat?" I said, elbowing him.

Victor beamed. "Uncle Jorge will be confused but well pleased."

I put my head on his shoulder.

"I'm glad we're friends," I said to Victor.

I cringed. I meant to spout poetry, and instead, I friend-zoned him. I meant it, though. At first he was my crush, but now he had become a real person who kicked butt.

"Me too," Victor said.

I reached out and held his hand. Liz and Kevin sat next to Berna. Cassie and Curtis joined us too. Together, we watched Orgog sink into the ocean. Bubbles broke the ocean's surface, but then it was still and quiet. The giant was asleep.

Curtis blinked. "Whoa. I had the strangest dream."

Cassie looked into his eyes. "Curtish? Ish that you?"

Curtis rubbed his forehead. "Dude. That was one strange trip."

We exhaled with relief. Cassie pinched Curtis's cheek. "Don't do that again."

The DC-3 buzzed overhead. The Nanny Brigade had patched up the wing and were following the yacht, keeping watch on the ship full of precious cargo.

The ocean was smooth and calm in the twilight. There would be major fallout to come from my parents. *Serious* consequences. But for now, I let the sea spray blow across my face and wash the soot and mud and filth of Sunshine Island from my cheeks.

"If this is what Valentine's Day is like every year, then count me in," Liz said.

Victor let out a big sigh.

"What's wrong?" I asked him.

"If all we are is friends, does that mean you won't go to the dance with me?"

I shot straight up.

"Finally!" I shouted at the top of my lungs.

"Is that yes?" Victor asked.

I was about to scream an earsplitting "Yes!" when I stopped.

"Sorry, Victor. I already said I'd go with Berna," I said.

"Don't be silly, Ferguson," Berna said. "Go with your boy."

"I made you a promise, and I'm going to keep it," I said.

Berna rolled her eyes. "Victor, you can come with us, too," she said.

"A triple date? With you and Kelly?" Victor said excitedly. "Excellent!"

Everyone laughed except for Kevin.

The Nanny Brigade returned the nineteen kids to their parents. There were tearful reunions. Every family was stunned when their nasty girl or bad boy rushed into their arms and promised to be good from that moment forward. They would do their chores. They would mow the lawn. They'd take out the trash.

Their parents didn't care about chores. They were just happy to have their children back.

The fifty monster mutants were a little more difficult. They were all totally cool; it was the rest of the world we were afraid about. Under the cover of night, they were taken to a refuge in upstate New York, some secret place in the Adirondacks called the Orion

Center, where the kids could roam and play and be free while the babysitters gently broke the news to their parents around the world and researched ways to reverse their transformations.

My parents met us at the docks when we arrived. They ran to me.

"Don't you ever do that again!" my mother screamed, holding me tight.

"Sorry, Mom. Sorry, Dad," I said.

I felt comfort in their arms. Safe. I could sleep for a thousand years like my homeboy Orgog.

Mama Vee told them everything we had done. How we bravely rescued fifty mutants, nineteen lost children, and saved the world.

"Sweet angel," said Elder Pressbury, taking my mother's shaking hands. "Your child is very special."

"I know that," my mother said.

Pressbury's voice fell to a deep hush. "There are dark forces in this world, my dear. Some so evil, I cannot begin to describe them to you without unsettling your heart. But your daughter has a gift that the world needs at this very moment."

I cocked my head. Was this the same lady who had publically destroyed me three days ago?

The three Elders reached out. Each of them stacked their hands upon my mother's hand.

"You have done a wonderful job with her," said Pressbury.

My mom's anger immediately switched targets.

"Just a second, ladies," my mom said. "The last time I saw you, you were ripping my kid to shreds. Now you want to sing her praises? You're not getting off that easy."

I smiled as my dad stood by my mother's side. The Elders looked shocked. They'd apologized for not believing in me, but my mom wasn't having it.

"I want to talk colleges for Kelly right now," she insisted. "I want to see paperwork, not just promises. We're talking full ride here."

The Elders stuttered and agreed with my Big Bad Mom.

I still ended up grounded for three months. But I made an agreement with my parents: I could go to the Valentine's Day dance for one hour. It was a tough negotiation, what with me running away and risking my life, but my mother and father agreed that I deserved to go to the dance in exchange for stopping Orgog the Annihilator and Baron von Eisenvult. If you ever want to get out of severe parental punishment: save the world. It works wonders.

"One hour," my mom said to me in the car. "We will be parked right here, and if you make a break for it, we will chase you down."

"Thank you for letting me do this," I said, adjusting the shoulders of my poufy pink dress. "Is this okay? I have to be color coordinated with Berna and Victor."

"You look beautiful," my mother said. "How's the arm?"

I smiled and held up my cast. We had bedazzled it with rhinestones to match my dress.

"Feeling superdorky right about now. I feel like I overdid it with the hair spray."

"You look like a little lady," my mother said. Her voice was getting emotional. "I don't know how you do what you do, Kelly."

"I couldn't do it without your help. Love you, Mom. Love you, Dad. But the clock's ticking," I said.

"You keep a foot between you and Victor. I'm serious. Measure it or I will!" my dad said.

I scrambled out of the car and approached our middle school gymnasium. I had dreamed about moments like this. Watched them in a bazillion romantic movies. And now, I, Kelly Ferguson, was going to my first dance.

Nerves ballooned inside me as I stood in line to buy my ticket. Berna was waiting for me by the door, holding a red ticket and a small bouquet of flowers. I smiled

WILLOW BROOK MIDDLE SCHOOL
VALENTINE'S DAY DANCE
FEATURING DJ MEGA SAUCE
♥ ♥ $10 ♥ ♥

and handed her a teddy bear clutching a little heart that said "I wuv you" when it was squeezed.

Victor joined us both. He had on a thin tie and a burgundy suit on.

"Your man looks fly," Berna whispered.

I bit my lip as he approached.

"You look like a dream," he said to me.

My cheeks flushed with fire.

He bowed like royalty to me and to Berna. "And so do you, Berna."

Berna smiled.

"But we must hurry! My parents went loco. I'm grounded for life. They have let me come to the dance for an hour, and that only was after Mama Vee and the Elders informed them of our brave deeds."

"Me too," I said.

"For real? My mom was psyched! Let's not waste any more time!" Berna said.

We linked arms and walked into the sound of a heartbreaking, awesome pop song. The kind that memories are made of. A disco ball spun from the ceiling. Streamers and a few heart posters hung on the walls. DJ Mega Sauce was playing all the hits.

But no one was dancing.

Kids from grades six through eight stood around the dance floor like zombies. Willow Brook Middle School was not a party.

I dragged my friends to the dance floor. The three of us jumped and bopped like lunatics while everyone watched from the sidelines. Cassie pulled Curtis to the dance floor, and we all jumped around. We did the chicken, the Floss, the Beyoncé flip, the Dougie, the Carlton and, of course, the Monster Mash. We even turned a few babysitter fight moves into dance moves: the Nanny Bounce, the Sitter Swag, and the Babysitter Bop.

Deanna and the Princess Pack snorted at us. I didn't care. It felt good to be stupid and free with my friends. A few months ago I would have been too shy and too quiet to do this in public, but after riding the shoulder of an ancient monster the size of a mountain, the middle school dance was no big deal. It was just a gymnasium that smelled like sweat socks and cupcakes. I wanted to celebrate with my friends. Who cared about their comments, good or bad? Seeing our courage, the rest of the school joined in and danced around us.

A slow song came on.

And now, for the moment we've all been waiting for.

Victor and I slow danced with our arms extended, leaving a little space between us. The music swirled, and everything was perfect.

"You're the real deal, Victor," I said.

We didn't talk for the rest of the song. The space closed between us, and I leaned my head on his shoulder.

An upbeat song started, and even though I didn't want to let go, it was getting weird with me hanging on to his neck while everyone else was jumping around. We decided to take a break. He escaped to the bathroom, and I got some cherry punch with Berna, Cassie, and Curtis.

"We need Victor in the order, stat," Curtis said. "He's a true American hero."

Cassie nodded. "He shaved our shkin."

"He's going to hate Heck Weekend," I said with a smile.

"Please tell me that boy goes to our school," Berna said. She was gazing over her cup at a tall, muscular kid with long, shaggy brown hair in his eyes who was wearing a T-shirt and jeans. He looked vaguely familiar.

"He's cute," I whispered. "Go say hi."

"He's so Gosling," Berna sighed.

"Looks like he's in high school," Curtis said.

"He'sh not even dresshed up. What'sh he doing here?"

"Looks lost," I said.

Berna's eyes widened. "He's coming over here!"

"Be cool!" I said.

We all swung around and turned our backs to him.

"Hey, guys," said buff, shaggy guy.

Berna and I exchanged glances. Is the guy with the huge biceps really talking to us?

"Do we know you?" I said nervously.

The stranger tucked his long, messy hair behind his ear and gave me a small, nervous smile.

My heart stopped. "Kevin?" I whispered.

The tall stranger nodded.

"No freaking way," Curtis said.

"How?" Berna asked.

Kevin shook his head in disbelief. "Professor Gonzalo squawked. The babysitters kept him in their custody, and Pressbury broke him down. He told them everything. My tail's almost gone, and most of my fur's fallen off."

He lifted his T-shirt, showing us patches of fur on his back.

"That means Hudson and all those kids are okay?" I asked.

"All thanks to you," he said. His gaze never left my face.

My eyes flooded as I imagined Hudson and all the monster kids being delivered safely back to their families. The lost kids of Sunshine Island were finally going home. Hope and joy welled up inside of me, and I couldn't stop the happy tears from spilling down my cheeks.

"I'm sorry. I didn't mean to make you cry," Kevin said.

I smiled. "It's okay. I'm so happy you're here."

I threw my arms around him and held him close. Liz popped up from under the bleachers. She was wearing a leather jacket, a shredded skirt, and pink combat boots. She stood at her brother's side.

"Yo, guys. Figured security would be tight here so Kevin and I snuck in. I see you've re-met. Crazy, huh? Even though I thought he was cool the way he was," Liz said, messing up Kevin's hair.

"I wanted to do it," Kevin said, rubbing the back of his neck.

"Why?" I asked. "You were awesome. Trouble. But awesome."

"I did it so I could do this," he said quietly.

He leaned forward. I closed my eyes.

Slurp! Kevin licked the side of my cheek with his slobbering tongue. Everyone laughed. I wiped the drool off my cheek and playfully shoved him.

Same old Kevin. Nothing but trouble.

Victor came back and joined us. He looked at Kevin, a little suspicious. "Who's this guy?" Victor asked.

"Bro!" Kevin grabbed Victor into a huge bear hug. "That was pretty cool, you going up in that slingshot," said Kevin.

Victor's eyebrows jumped.

Kevin let out a funny "arroo."

Victor bro-hugged Kevin. "You look amazing, man!"

Kevin grinned. "Thanks. I've waited so long to be able to say this out loud."

He nervously wiped his hands on his jeans. "Wow. Okay. Sorry I got you suspended. I never meant to get you in trouble. I was only trying to look out for you. Because whenever I felt lonely and lost, I thought about you guys. You're my friends. And you have no idea how much you mean to me."

"I think I know," I said.

"Let's dance, losers!" Liz shouted.

Liz, Berna, Cassie, and Curtis leaped into a circle. Victor, Kevin, and I joined them, and I watched the best babysitters in the world whirl and laugh with wild, celebratory abandon. Yes, there would be more monsters, more bumps in the night, more battles, more drama, more broken bones and great sacrifices. I would probably need counseling for the rest of my life to get the haunting image of the Wolf out of my head. And pretty soon, we would face the biggest horror show of them all: high school.

But for now, we were a bunch of goofballs, dancing together. The world was ours. Anything was possible.

ACKNOWLEDGMENTS

The book's over. Why are you still reading? Are you one of *those* people who just see words and need to read them? Hopefully you're still reading because you had such a good time that you want to hang and chat like the movie just let out and we're gathered in the theater lobby all abuzz. So, what did you think of *Mission to Monster Island*? Really? That's fascinating! Sorry, I didn't mean to interrupt. Ah, yes, that is a bit of a plot hole, but please don't tell anyone else.

Great, now let's all go get some ice cream and I'll tell you about the incredible people who helped build this rickety roller coaster.

First up, editor Maria Barbo. Maria has been through three giant Boogeypeople battles with me and has always led us to victory. Maria enthusiastically loves our gang of monster hunters so much I think she might be one herself. In Maria's backpack you will find an assortment of weapons, such as a proofreading dog, a character nuance amulet, and a very sharp machete for pacing. Writers are like toddlers in the rain, prone to splashing in muddy puddles and making a huge mess of themselves. Assistant editor Stephanie Guerdan, aka the Great Guerdan, had to organize that mess, and I doubt you would be reading this were it not for her wondrous train-conducting skills. All hail the Great Guerdan! Vivienne To's ability to translate my words into super cool pictures, her endless creativity, and talent always wow me. Which drawing is your favorite? My favorite one is—all of them. I'm constantly amazed at the teamwork that goes into getting this very book into your hands. There are copy editors, art editors, marketing people, the big boss, Katherine Tegen, and an entire room of elves that paint each book cover. Thank you for your hard work and your time making these books a reality.

The very first people to hear any of my stories were my parents. I would tell them tales about giant rats living in sewers and superheroes, and they always encouraged me—even though I am sure those stories needed some serious proofreading. My folks are a huge reason why I am able to do what I do and I am forever thankful to them for being a kind, supportive first audience. They did more than listen, too. They played with me and let me be a weird kid without trying to change me. So thanks, Mom and Dad.

I do my best to keep my work in the workshop but it follows me through the walls like a ghostly haunt, whispering sentences and ideas every waking moment. My darling, dearest Cara is with me in the spooky darkness, knowing when to fend off the ghosts and when to welcome them to tea. She fills my heart and soul every day. Our life together with our son has never been better.

And yes, all that mushy stuff helps when writing a book—except when Theo wanders into my office and draws on my manuscript pages with blueberry yogurt. Thanks, kiddo.

Hopefully the next time we meet we'll be talking about book four and the movie of book one.

What's that? A movie?! Ah. That is an entirely different story for another time. Thank you for riding the rides on Monster Island with me, my friends. I suppose now is a good time to tell you that I am terrified of roller coasters.

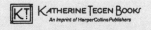